The Prayer Shawl Chronicles

Stories of Unlikely Connections & Unexpected Gifts

By Cynthia Coe

D1377871

The Prayer Shawl Chronicles: Stories of Unlikely Connections & Unexpected Gifts

ISBN: 9781975652340

Published by Sycamore Cove Creations

Sycamore Cove
Creations
Knoxville

www.sycamorecove.org

www.sycamorecoveknitting.com

For information, permissions, or to contact the author, please email sycamorecovecreations@gmail.com

Introduction

What's A Prayer Shawl?

Knit with love, prayer shawls offer a tangible sign of prayer for those in need of comfort, healing, or special concern. Knitters spend hours of steady work crafting a piece of fabric from yarn that embodies their hopes and blessings, their prayers spoken or silent.

Prayer shawls come in all colors, sizes, and shapes. There are no rules governing prayer shawls. Sometimes a knitter may choose bright colors to offer cheer, warm colors to offer comfort, or a long, oversized blanket style shawl to use in a hospital or on a sick bed. Smaller prayer shawls might comfort a child or a pet. It might ride along in the purse, backpack, or suitcase of a traveler, student, or just someone facing everyday worries and concerns.

Crafters of prayer shawls may know the person who receives their lovingly created cloth. They may only know the recipient as an acquaintance who struggles through a crisis or needs healing of one kind or another. Often, knitters donate their prayer shawls anonymously, trusting that their work from the heart and the hands will end up comforting a person in need of some kind, someone they might never meet.

My Story

I knitted my first prayer shawl for my father shortly after he moved into a nursing home specializing in dementia. I knitted a huge, hospital bed sized blanket in browns and gold. Every stitch bore my love, my grief for his condition, and my hopes that he would find love and care in his last years of life. The nursing home staff carefully draped this oversized prayer shawl over my father's bed each and every day, knowing it carried his daughter's thoughts and prayers.

Knitting prayer shawls became my therapy during my father's two year stay in the nursing home. I shared several of my subsequent prayer shawls with some of my father's "neighbors" in the dementia ward of the nursing home. Most of them struggled to speak coherently, but their smiles and eyes showed me how profoundly they appreciated the gift of a huge, fuzzy blanket made just for them.

Eventually, my life returned to a more normal (but often stressful) routine of raising three children. But I kept knitting prayer shawls, donating them to the healing ministry of my church.

Every Prayer Shawl Has Two Stories

In donating prayer shawls anonymously, I quickly learned that there are at least two great stories behind every prayer shawl – the story of the crafter, and the story of the recipient. Though these two people are connected by one prayer shawl, they may have vastly different stories. The knitting craftsperson who spends hours making a prayer shawl and the man or woman who receives it may never meet or have anything in common. They may never cross each other's paths.

The handcrafter knits each stitch in the silence of "alone time" with God, or perhaps in a weekly or monthly meeting of a knitting guild or other group time spent with kindred souls. A knitter might simply need to take time for healing of her own troubles, sorrows, or crises. The Prayer Shawl becomes a tangible symbol of this healing time spent in prayer and fellowship. Once another person receives it, his or her journey becomes looped around and tied to that of the knitter, just as yarn is looped around and secured to make an intricate piece of fabric – a new design that is so much more than that single strand of yarn that started the whole thing.

I hope you enjoy these stories of women who knit prayer shawls and those who receive them. Each one is a fictional tale of someone who finds herself in need of healing - and how that quest for healing ultimately helps someone else heal as well. Unexpected gifts appear, seemingly out of nowhere. Unlikely connections are made, sometimes across cultures and even continents, sometimes between people who might never imagine themselves connected in any way – just like the work of the Holy Spirit itself.

Blessings,
Cynthia Coe

Sycamore Cove Farm
Knoxville, Tennessee

Table of Contents

Blessing of the Prayer Shawls

All Ginger knew of All Saints Church was the Healing Garden where she walked her dog in the afternoons. And that it was safe. As she followed her golden retriever, Gus, along the mulchy path through the redbud and dogwood trees, a rain drop plopped down on her nose. She winced, feeling her fragile sense of security evaporating.

She zipped her raincoat and flipped the hood over her greying red hair. She hoped her scuffed sneakers, the only shoes left from her former life, would hold up through one more rainstorm.

Ginger and her husband Steve had fled the Houston area after the last hurricane destroyed their old Victorian home with the wraparound porch, flooding the meadow of wildflowers surrounding it and then seeping into the ground floor. The insurance adjuster called it a total loss and added that it would likely happen again. So they headed for the hills, literally. Ginger had gone to college in Knoxville, and the memory of the Smoky Mountains looming over the outskirts of the horizon immediately came to mind when faced with the reality of losing her home in the meadow for good.

"Come on, Gus, let's get out of this rain." She pulled on the leash and led her dog out through the gates of the Healing Garden, thinking they could stand

1

in the shelter of the church's arched stone walkway running alongside the flower beds until this early spring pop-up shower passed on.

A woman holding a basket of colorful pieces of fabric stepped outside the double red doors of the grey stone church and looked up at the sky. She wore a crisp white and blue-striped shirtdress and sensible leather flats. Her grey-white hair looked as if she had just visited the beauty shop, and her make-up looked freshly applied. Noticing Ginger coming towards her, she waved.

Ginger waved back, making note – too late – of a sign posted outside the church building, "Blessing of the Prayer Shawls, Today at Noon." She winced. Getting roped into attending a church service was not on her agenda. She just wanted a temporary shelter.

"Come on in!" the woman standing at the church door beckoned to Ginger.

Ginger tugged on the leash to reign in Gus and convinced herself to at least speak politely to the woman. "Thanks, but we just wanted to get out of the rain."

"That's fine. But you're welcome to come on in to the service," the woman said.

Ginger stepped closer to the church door to get under the archway framing the bright red church door. Her athletic shoes squished with rainwater, and she had water stains covering her jeans. Gus began to shake his fur again, and Ginger quickly patted him in an effort to protect the church lady's white dress.

"I have my dog with me. We just came from a walk."

Melba Strickland took one long look at the forty-something woman standing before her and made an executive decision on behalf of her church. "Bring him inside. Today, we allow dogs into the church service." She smiled, seeing the surprise on the younger woman's face. "I wish I had brought my dog today! He would have enjoyed having a play date."

"If you're sure you don't mind…." The rain had turned into a deluge. Ginger didn't look forward to standing around the church courtyard for what looked like a set-in rain storm. And she hadn't brought her phone with her to call for a ride.

"It's fine. Really." Melba, remembering her basket of pocket prayer shawls, as well as her intention to offer one to each person attending the service today. "And here, this is for you." She handed Ginger a small rectangle of knitted fabric. "This orange one matches your hair." She glanced down at the canine sniffing the hem of her dress. "And your dog as well."

Ginger accepted the small piece of cloth. "What is it?"

"It's a prayer shawl. A tiny one. A prayer shawl you can keep in your pocket, or in your purse," Melba told her.

"A prayer shawl?"

"You'll see. Now go on in and take a seat."

Ginger stepped inside the semi-darkened church. Candles stood on either side of a heavy oak table in the front, and several large, colorful, fuzzy blankets had been stacked on top of it. A fuzzy purple blanket overlapped a green, intricately lace-patterned triangular shawl. An orange blanket served as a runner underneath a silver plate and chalice, and over the front of the table a cream-colored blanket peeked out.

Even more of the colorful blankets were draped over a railing between the oak table and the church pews. To the left, a long, narrow blue and red striped piece of knitting hung down almost to the floor, with larger blankets in red, pink, mustard yellow, and navy blue placed over the entire left side of the railing. On the right side of the church, a delicate grey blanket anchored the display of what the woman called "prayer shawls" on the waist-high railing, along with chunkier blankets in spring green, a multi-colored pattern of forest green and blue, and several skinny pieces that looked as if they could be winter scarves.

Ginger took a seat in the back pew, with Gus following behind to collapse on the floor for a nap. Ten or so other ladies, all of them considerably older than Ginger, silently entered the church and took seats in pews nearer the front. Smiles were exchanged, but no one spoke.

Ginger settled into the comfortable silence, glad to have a warm, dry place to take shelter. The dark wood of the pew felt solid. The rainbow in the stained glass directly behind the heavy oak table in the front of the church reminded her that flooding, as bad as it could be, eventually ended.

She clutched the small patch of knitted fabric in her hand. Gus's wet dog smell wafted up through the smell of burning candle wax, but no one seemed to mind. Maybe this wouldn't be so bad after all, Ginger thought.

The Rev. Will Henderson took a deep breath as the organist kicked off his favorite hymn, "Hail Thee Festival Day." The ladies of the Knitting Guild had questioned use of such an exuberant song for such a small service, but Will had assured them that even a small event warranted a joyful noise, even if sung by only a dozen voices.

The deacon, Martha Craig, stepped off in procession in front of him, holding the ornate red and gold-embossed Gospel, while she in turn followed Harold St. Martin, the elderly man who always volunteered to serve as crucifer. Harold had told Will it made him feel useful, carrying the cross in and out of the weekday healing service held each week. Will had winced at the notion of having to find tasks just to feel useful. At age fifty-six and with silver hair and creaky knees, he would find himself retired and possibly struggling for relevance sooner than he'd like to acknowledge.

As Martha and Harold approached the altar and stepped off to their seats on the side of the church, the prayer shawls draped over the altar and the altar railings on both sides of the chapel came into full view. Will smiled. The colors alone lifted his mood.

Turning to face the small congregation at the front of the nave, he silently counted heads. As a rector, his job entailed making sure enough folks showed up to justify his time and the church's money. At least that's what he told himself. Really, he would have showed up to lead the weekly healing service in the small chapel even if only a handful of old ladies showed up. He needed the close connections he made when he knelt to pray with each person who came to him with their most heartfelt prayers.

The Knitting Guild ladies had hoped a dozen parishioners would attend their annual Blessing of the Prayer Shawls. Will had cautioned them to simply appreciate each and every soul in attendance, rather than focus on numbers. Nevertheless, he noted with satisfaction a new and, at forty-ish years old, a much younger woman joining the service for the first time. He did not see the woman's dog on the floor of his church.

As the organist played the final strains of the opening hymn, Will walked to the center of the chapel. "Welcome! Today we celebrate the Blessing of the Prayer Shawls. Let us pray."

"Lord," he continued, "We gather here today to ask your blessings upon these prayer shawls. Bless the hands that crafted them, and bless those who will deliver them to hospitals, nursing homes, and to anyone in need of healing and prayer. We ask your blessings on each and every person who receives a prayer shawl. Help each to know he or she is loved and held in prayer by our faith community. In Christ's name, Amen."

A handful of worshipers mumbled "amen," and Will took his seat off to the side of the chapel while Harold and Martha read the scripture passages for the day. His mind drifted off to the thoughts of questioning his most recent call as Harold read the familiar words of the twenty-third Psalm. Picturing that dark valley of death in the Psalm, he pictured himself in a dark valley, stepping forward in faith yet not knowing where he would end up.

Every time he found himself in a church meeting – or any kind of church gathering, for that matter – Will felt constrained, as if someone had pushed him down into a box. He found his mind questioning whether ministry had to happen within the wall of the church building, whether he should step outside into the wider world to follow his call.

His divorce had made him question everything about himself – his ability to maintain any relationship, his looks, his sense of humor, his intelligence, even his call to the ordained ministry. His bishop had told him this was normal, but that didn't exactly help. In the old days, Will reminded himself, divorce of a priest would result in shame, scandal, and probable assignment to a new parish. Of course, maybe he needed a fresh start, he mused. Even though his wife had moved out of town with her new husband, every day he sensed that every congregant he encountered would silently wonder what Sandy had found so lacking in him that she had walked out on him without so much as a goodbye.

Will forced himself to focus on the scripture readings. He had a homily prepared, short remarks extolling the virtues of pastoral care by the laity, those valiant souls who worked for the church without pay and often without recognition. He believed those remarks a little more than he should, failing to say anything positive about his own ministry as a priest. He made a note to watch what he said. If he slipped up and gave these folks reason to think he even considered a call to leave the priesthood, he feared he would lose his job quickly and not exactly on his own terms and at his own pace – not to mention God's own perfect timing.

He glanced over at Melba Strickland, holding down her position in the front pew. She served on the vestry at the moment and would listen carefully and report back to the rest of the church's governing body if he even hinted at a personal dilemma.

Focus on the prayer shawls, Will counseled himself. Harold read off the Prayers of the People, and Will silently prayed for the recipient of each prayer shawl draped across the altar rail.

As he turned his attention to Martha, who had risen to read the Gospel, Will tried to imagine where these prayer shawls would end up. Each would end up as part of a story, some of them with happy endings, stories of healing and peace. Some would end up wrapping someone inconsolable, someone beyond any sort of human help. Some might simply get stowed in a closet or tossed off as one more thing someone didn't particularly want. You never knew.

Martha held up the Gospel book after reading the story of Jesus's own home congregation trying to throw him off a cliff. The story always gave Will an odd sort of reassurance. Maybe it was the way Jesus calmly walked away from all the angry tension in the crowd.

When he opened his mouth to give his homily, he found himself beginning a sermon he had not planned. "When I was in college, I often heard a song by The Clash: 'Should I Stay or Should I Go?' Friends, this is often the question we ask of God."

Will deftly blended these words into an exploration of whether the prayer shawls knitted by the ladies' guild would do more good draped over the altar or draped around the arms of a person in need. Glancing over at Melba Strickland, who listened attentively with a slight smile on her face, he assured himself that he had recovered nicely from almost saying what really weighed on his mind.

The silver-haired priest with the piercing blue eyes startled Ginger with his mention of The Clash. Coming of age in the eighties, she had gone to one of their concerts as a student at the University of Tennessee long ago. Perhaps this was a sign from God, Ginger wondered? Much to her own surprise, she listened with rapt attention to this priest who looked like he could be a senior partner in a law firm in her old world in corporate Houston. Why would anyone as articulate and intelligent as this seemingly type-A man devote his life to a church full of old ladies, she wondered?

The silver-haired preacher spoke of living in a broken world, of dealing with everyday crap and injustices, of crises you find yourself in and never saw coming. The look in his eyes told Ginger that he knew of what he spoke. And what should you do about all these calamities? Should you stay or should you go?

Ginger leaned forward to listen to the answer. She reached down to stroke her dog's still damp fur, reaching to touch the one creature besides her husband still in her life after the flood. Should she have stayed there? Did she pull a major cop-out by heading for the hills?

"Should you stay or should you go?" the priest continued. "My friends, the answer is yours to discern. It's not for me to tell you what to do. It's not for you to tell me what to do, either."

At this, the woman in the front row made a nervous chortling sound. Several of the other ladies in the congregation simply smiled. The rector himself paused to smile as well, as if to signal his good humor at the notion of these elderly people giving him marching orders.

"What are you leaving, and where are you going? That is the answer to following God's will for us after disaster, pain, or any misfortune, my friends. Can you make a difference where you are, or are you better off serving God and others someplace else?"

The rector paused, as if reflecting on his own questions. No one in the small, dark chapel moved as the questions hung in the air, punctuated only by the flicker of the two tall candles on the large oak table behind the priest.

Ginger stared at the neat rows of stitching on the little patch of knitting she still held in her hand. The priest's questions hurt. In times of trouble, she had often fled places of pain for exotic, distracting adventures in other lands. She and Steve had wanted children early in their marriage, but children never came. So they spent their free time and money travelling the globe – the more remote and exotic, the better. Glancing around the candle-lit church, Ginger thought back to their trip across Europe back in the nineties. They had backpacked from Amsterdam to the Urals, with only a small backpack each to haul a change of clothes and a toothbrush. They had crossed the Iron Curtain in the days right after the Berlin Wall fell, taken an old Soviet train from East Berlin, ending up in a shabby hotel in Moscow.

Right before they returned home to Houston, they had visited the colorful and surreal nine domed St. Basil's Cathedral across from Red Square, and she had felt a sense of mystical union with the divine for the first time. But then, back home in Texas, she had never felt that way again. She had marked the experience down to the swirling colors of the cathedral, fatigue, and gratefulness for a life of adventure and a husband as daring as she to explore the unknown. She had never entered a church since then.

"Should I stay or should I go?" The question nagged at Ginger as everyone in the chapel rose to their feet and began to recite words out of small red books. No one noticed her, still in her seat in the back, so she

11

simply sat and listened. Glancing back towards the door of the chapel, she thought about grabbing Gus's collar and slipping out the back. No one would notice, and she wouldn't have to make conversation or participate in whatever would come next in the church service.

But she stayed. Maybe, she thought, I've been too quick to cut and run from my troubles, my disasters, my plain bad luck.

She watched the elderly ladies plod up to the front of the church to kneel down and receive a small piece of bread and a sip of red wine. She wondered if by simply watching, she intruded on them somehow. But somehow, she felt completely comfortable nestled against the solid wood of the back pew of the church, keeping watch over her dog as he took a nice snooze.

As the parishioners returned to their seats, Ginger tucked the little piece of orange knitting into the pocket of her raincoat. She didn't want to lose it.

Martha Craig hung back, ostensibly tidying up the altar, as the parishioners meandered and chatted after the healing service. She still wore her long, white robe and deacon's sash. She had never enjoyed small talk. She worked better with people who wanted to engage in substantial discussion. As her friend Melba socialized down by the chapel door, Martha enjoyed a few minutes of quiet before re-engaging with the rest of humanity.

Picking up the chalice to empty the leftover wine, Martha glanced back towards the door of the chapel. A younger woman with greying strawberry-blond hair stayed huddled in the back pew, watching the others greet the rector and take their leave.

A new person out of her element, Martha thought. She placed the chalice back on the altar and lumbered to the back pew to greet the young woman. "Good to see you here today. I'm Martha, the deacon."

The young woman, still wearing a rain speckled coat from an earlier thunderstorm before the service, took her hand but looked bemused. Martha often got that reaction from non-churchy people.

"I'm Ginger. We're just taking shelter from the rain. But I'm glad we stayed."

"We?"

Martha followed Ginger's eyes down to the floor, where a big golden-brown dog with matted fur raised his head, tongue hanging out. "Oh! I didn't realize…that's why you didn't come to the Communion rail," she said, mostly to herself.

No one had ever dared bring a dog to the healing service. As the last of the ladies exited the nave and chatted with Will, Martha stepped around to block their view of the dog.

"Well, we're glad you joined us today." She stooped to pet the dog's head. "What's his name?"

"Gus. We usually take our midday walks in the garden beside the church."

"Good to hear. Several of us fought hard to get that garden put in and open to the public."

"It's wonderful. I appreciate the church letting us use it."

Martha noticed one of Melba's "pocket prayer shawls" peeking out of Ginger's coat pocket. Martha had scoffed at her friend's idea of making miniature prayer shawls out of leftover yarn. But that was Melba, always wanting to try out elaborate ideas she found in her decorating and crafting magazines.

"I see you got one of the Prayer Patches. We usually don't have all those things piled up on the altar like this. Join us again, and it won't look so garish up at the altar."

"It's a sweet idea," Ginger replied. She pulled the little piece of knitting from her pocket and held it, like a young child holding on to a security blanket. Martha noted this and decided maybe her friend's idea of handing out mini-shawls might not be so crazy after all.

The golden retriever on the floor, awakened by the conversation, pulled itself to standing and sniffed around the bottom of Martha's robe. Still damp from the rainstorm, his fur left greyish-brown spots on her pristine white vestment.

"Gus, no!" Ginger grabbed her dog's collar and tried to pull him back.

"It's fine," Martha told. She bent to pet the dog on the head. "Ministry gets messy sometimes."

Ginger looked up at her, not knowing quite what to make of that statement.

"You know you're welcome back any time," Martha told her.

"Thank you," Ginger replied.

Martha watched as the red-headed woman led her dog out of the nave, stopping to shake hands with the rector on her way out. She made no further apologies for the dog and let the beast lick the rector's face as he reached down to ruffle the dog's head.

"I admire that kind of moxy," Martha said to herself. She wondered if she would ever see the young woman again.

After all the parishioners had left, Martha changed out of her white robe, glad to relax in her familiar and oversized grey sweat pants and sweatshirt. Finding clothes to fit her large frame was always a challenge, and at some point, she had given up. All vanities anyway, she told herself.

On her way out, she found Father Will gathering up and stacking the brightly colored prayer shawls.

"Ready to go out into the world, huh?" she asked him.

He startled and stared at her.

"The prayer shawls? Ready to go to new homes, is what I meant."

Will stared at her for a moment longer. "Yes, I suppose you're right."

Martha patted him on the back. She had always liked Father Henderson. She felt sorry for him, after his wife seemingly found herself married to the church instead of him and left, presumably, to save any iota of her own identity she could still find within herself. Probably what he was thinking with all that business about "should I stay or should I go" in his homily. But you never knew what was going on in somebody else's head…or in their life, she had learned long ago.

Martha gave a final goodbye pat to a large shawl she had knitted herself with thick, bulky yarn and huge cables down the sides. "I'm sure each one of these will go out into the world and bring lots of comfort to someone special."

Father Henderson glanced over the row of prayer shawls and nodded. "And each one will have a story to tell." He left the prayer shawls and his deacon at the altar, deep in his own thoughts. He had decisions to make.

Smells and Bells

Will finished hanging up his vestments in the small room behind the nave, having greeted the handful of parishioners who had attended the Blessing of the Prayer Shawls. By the time he stepped into the nave again, he found himself alone in the dark, grey-stone silence of the empty worship space. The church had been designed to look like a country chapel in nineteenth century England, but with air conditioning for the hot, humid southern climate of Tennessee. Will glanced up towards the rafters, noting that the shape of the nave looked like an upside-down ark, a boat turned upside down. As the rain lightly battered the roof overhead, Will hoped the roof wouldn't leak and cause yet another financial crisis he'd had to deal with.

As soon as he pushed open the back door and turned right into the church's slightly more modern office suite, any peace he had found within the silent nave vanished. The receptionist held up a fistful of pink "while you were out" slips. His new associate priest stood frowning over the parish prayer list posted on the white board, her hands on her hips and a sour look on her face. Before he had a chance to take it all in, Cassandra, the parish housekeeper, came charging towards him with a long white robe in her arms. Will noted what looked like brown paw prints on the vestment, and he most definitely caught the whiff of a wet dog smell.

"Father Will, this I can't do," Cassandra firmly stated, pointing emphatically to the paw prints on the vestment. "Miss Martha has a funeral this afternoon, and there's no way I can get this clean and pressed in time."

The parish phone rang continually. The parish secretary marched off towards the ladies' room, ignoring the ringing phone.

Will sighed. The funerals in the parish had become so numerous that he had asked the deacon to handle half of them. The family of today's deceased had not requested Holy Communion and expected only a few mourners, so Martha had agreed to do the honors.

"I suppose there's not much we can do," he told Cassandra. Martha was so tall (and large as well) that the parish only had one garment she could wear while conducting services. Will considered sending the vestment out to the dry cleaners for an emergency cleaning, but he reminded himself that he needed to cut expenses to the bone.

The deacon had lumbered over to join the discussion. "That new lady had a dog. I needed to be friendly. It's not every day we get a new prospect, especially under the age of sixty."

"I know, I know," Will replied. "Look, here's what we'll do. I'll handle the funeral this afternoon. You take a break, Martha."

Cassandra nodded in satisfaction. "I'll soak it, have it ready for Sunday morning."

Martha nodded as well and turned to take an armful of prayer shawls Melba Strickland had brought in from the service, now neatly stacked and each tagged with a small card bearing the good wishes and prayers of All Saints Episcopal Church. Will reached to take his messages from the receptionist, noting that Abby, his young associate, had headed out the door, her professional leather handbag and two prayer shawls slung over her arm.

Will retreated to his office, congratulating himself for hiring Cassandra, thus killing several birds with one stone. Every year, it became harder and harder to find volunteers to serve on the altar guild, sign up for the kitchen guild, or take a shift on the church landscaping work group. The dwindling cadre of active parishioners who had called him as rector had aged into active seniors, then just plain elderly. None of them had the interest or stamina to take on the upkeep and maintenance that used to maintain a sense of community within the church.

The seventy-year-old ladies in the parish had collectively sighed with relief when he suggested hiring someone who actually needed a fulltime job to polish the silver patens and chalices, take care of all the vestments, and keep the kitchen clean. Will strategically waited until after the leftover casseroles in the parish kitchen accumulated a disturbing pink slime until he made this suggestion. When he took the further step of hiring a refugee from Honduras, he could also report to his bishop that he had fulfilled Christ's call to minister to the poor and those without a home.

Cassandra had worked for the church for the past five years and hadn't missed a day of work. She dutifully - if not cheerfully - kept the parish clean, the refrigerator cleared of aged casserole dishes, the priests' robes spotlessly white and crisply ironed, the parish office dusted and vacuumed, and the pews polished and free of leftover bulletins. She balked, however, at going outside on hot, humid days to weed the flower gardens. Will eventually let her out of these duties. Cassandra had enough to do, and he frankly didn't want to lose her to another employer. He paid a landscaper out of discretionary funds and hoped the church gardens didn't get too far out of hand.

Will sighed and sat down at his desk to finalize his proposed budget for the church vestry. Thinking about how Cassandra looked increasingly tired and overworked, he included a modest part-time salary for an outdoor groundskeeper and janitor for the next year. With many of the parishioners approaching eighty years old, he couldn't count on a steady stream of cash donations to the collection plate to cover the landscaping forever. In fact, with the death of the old man whose body he would greet at the back of the church this afternoon, Will figured he was out another twenty bucks thrown in the plate each Sunday.

After three hours of trying to make the numbers work, Will shoved the draft budget into a file folder and prepared for the funeral. Stopping by the reception desk on the way back from the men's room, he pulled a nice blue and grey prayer shawl from the stack for presentation to the new widow. As an afterthought, he stepped back and picked out a prayer shawl for Cassandra, too. Unlike many employers, Will reminded himself, the church took an interest in the personal and spiritual wellbeing of the people who worked there. He considered himself Cassandra's shepherd, as much or maybe even more than he did the people who sat in the pews each Sunday.

Will folded the black, brown, and cream-colored prayer shawl into a neat bundle and wedged it into Cassandra's employee mail cubby. He wrote a note and tucked it within the folds of the fuzzy blanket. "Everyone here at All Saints appreciates everything you do for us. With deep gratitude, + Father Will."

Will stopped by his office once more to get the black leather-bound Bible and Book of Common Prayer he always carried during services. As he glanced out the window, he stopped and stared. A woman with long, wild, blondish-brown curls, vividly dressed in a flowing purple, yellow, and pink ankle-length dress slowly walked towards the church door in clunky leather sandals. He could hear the wood of her heels clop evenly across the asphalt, slowing as she approached the church entrance. She looked pensive, as if she had something on her mind.

He watched as she stopped at the door and briefly paused before reaching for the door handle. Within moments, he heard her sandals slowly clomp through the reception area. Will pondered whether he should step out of his office to greet her. But he had the sense she didn't want to be bothered. Probably here for the meeting for recovering addicts, Will speculated. He should respect her anonymity, he decided. But if he were honest, he found the woman fascinating. He wanted to meet her, but she also scared him for some reason. Maybe it was her slim, athletic figure underneath that flowy dress.

He waited in silence in his office as he heard her stop before opening the door to the hallway of meeting rooms and children's Sunday School rooms. Should he go out and say something to her after all? He waited. At this point, he didn't want to scare her or come across as some sort of stalker. Eventually, he heard the wooden heels of her sandals clomp off again, along with the swoosh of the door opening, the heels continuing and fading down the hall.

Will peeked out of his office. The woman had gone.

He ran a hand over his hair and turned to go to the funeral. Maybe he wasn't dead yet.

Newcomer's Ministry

Clarissa

"Just walk in there like you belong, Clarissa," I told myself. I hadn't crossed the door of a church since …when? Maybe as a four-year-old, before my folks split up and left us theologically adrift.

"I am who I am," I reassured myself as a I approached the glass doors at the back of the church. I just wanted to go to my meeting and not have to deal with any well-meaning church members. Yes, they would likely have a problem with my scruffy, free-form curls, which admittedly needed a trim, if not a good washing. Yes, they would likely turn their noses up at my outrageous floral hippy dress and clunky, scuffed sandals.

A sign directed me to the meeting I know I needed to attend for about the last year. I hadn't relapsed. But I felt close several times. Too close. Way too uncomfortably close.

To my slight disappointment, I found the church office empty as I passed by on my way to the meeting room down the hall. I stopped and listened. Yes, on a late Wednesday afternoon a church likely wouldn't be a beehive of activity. But still, I expected someone here to greet me, tell me I had come to the wrong place – something.

I spotted a bulletin board and paused to take a look. A few non-descript flyers announced a parish picnic (claiming "everyone welcome!"), a women's Bible study later that evening, and a notice by

23

somebody wanting to sell a used Honda. Then, in the lower corner, on a bright yellow piece of card stock, I noticed an appeal for something called prayer shawls. I stepped forward to read the details.

"Prayer shawls urgently needed! All sizes, colors, and styles welcome! Help our clergy minister to hospital patients and those in crisis by knitting or crocheting a prayer shawl for donation. Collection Box located in the church office."

I looked around and sure enough, I found a big cardboard box someone had decorated with bright yellow and white polka-dotted wrapping paper, with a sign over it, "Donations for Prayer Shawl Ministry."

I hadn't knitted for years. In my college days, I took my knitting needles to class, sat in the back of the lecture halls, and worked on afghans for my friends while the professor droned on. Once I traded a particularly nice green and brown blanket for a ride to the beach for spring break.

But after I finally got out of school and failed to get a job as an artist (like I really thought I could get a job with a degree in art) and ended up working at a women's shelter, trying to keep the peace and get everybody settled in and then moved on, the days of leisurely sitting around knitting had come to an end.

A shame, I thought, since I probably could have taught the gals in the women's shelter some coping skills that could have calmed them down – or at least given them something to do. I rummaged around in the donation box and inspected the donated prayer shawls the church members had left.

I could best all of these, I thought as I fingered the plain garter stitched blankets, some of them with obvious mistakes and holes in the patterns. I folded them carefully and headed on to my meeting.

Staying sober would be a pain in the butt, but I sucked it up and went through the familiar words and motions. "My name is Clarissa, and I'm a substance abuser."

I listened as well as I could to the others telling their stories, self-evaluating their progress. But I felt like I had time-warped back to my college days. My fingers itched for something to do. My mind preoccupied itself with a picture of a lovely blanket made in cashmere yarn of creams and yellows, adorned with delicate lacing all away around the edges.

On the way home, I stopped by the low-cost big box store and bought myself a pair of size eight circular needles on a long plastic cord and the best yarn I could afford in two shades of cream and three shades of pale yellows.

Several weeks later, the rector of the parish personally made a visit to Mrs. Eugenia Tyson. As a pillar of the church congregation, she would expect as much. The Reverend Will Henderson took a comb out of the visor of his old Mercedes to touch up his hair and brushed off the shoulders of his suit before stepping up to the ornate oak door of the small mansion.

Under his arm, he carried a tasteful and elaborately laced prayer shawl in intertwined shades of cream and yellow. He had gone through the donation box for the best of the lot. This particular piece of work had an intricate lace pattern, embroidered with whimsical yellow flowers – just the kind of high-quality artistry Mrs. Tyson would appreciate – depending on how much her eyesight had deteriorated.

A young woman opened the door and showed him into the River Room in the back of the spacious home. While waiting for Mrs. Tyson to appear, the rector enjoyed a perfect cup of coffee served in a china cup by the same young woman who ushered him in.

"Fah-thah Hen-da-son," Mrs. Tyson drawled as she pushed her walker through the River Room to a seating area for two, upholstered in chintz and overlooking the sparkling water below.

"Mrs. Tyson, so good to see you. Thank you for having me over."

Mrs. Tyson reached out to take the rector's proffered hand and squeezed it as hard as she could. The housekeeper followed behind her, bringing her a cup of tea and a pillow she wedged behind Mrs. Tyson's back.

The Rev. Henderson paused for a moment before presenting the parish's primary benefactress with the masterpiece in knitting he had managed to procure for her.

Mrs. Tyson reached to touch the prayer shawl. "Why Fatha Henda-son, that's just lovely." She ran her bony fingers over the lace edging, the delicate yellow flowers embroidered in perfect spacing. "Just lovely."

"Now who made this piece?"

Will Henderson knew better than to give the standard "all work is a gift to the glory of God" claim of anonymity the clergy usually gave when parishioners asked who had done the needlework.

"One of our newcomers, I believe," he cheerfully assured Mrs. Tyson. She would like that.

The old lady nodded in satisfaction. She had just written a check for $25,000 to fund an initiative to bring fresh young faces into her beloved church.

"That's fine, Fatha, just fine. Now she'll be coming over for my little soirée next month? I'd like to meet this fine person."

Shit, Will Henderson thought. He'd have to produce an actual person willing to confess to knitting the lovely prayer shawl. "Of course, Mrs. Tyson. I'm sure we'll have a fine crop of new folks to introduce." He hoped to God he could get at least ten people through the door.

"That's fine. Very fine." She spread the prayer shawl over her lap, continuing to finger each of the delicate bright yellow flowers. "I know someone put much work into this piece. Such a blessing."

The Rev. Henderson nodded. "Shall I pray with you, Mrs. Tyson?"

She nodded. A small tear ran down her old face. She made no attempt to hide it or wipe it away.

"Dear Lord, we give thanks for the love and dedication woven into this prayer shawl and pray it will comfort Eugenia and give her a deep sense of peace. Help her to know that each stitch has been knitted with the love of one of our parishioners on behalf of all your flock at All Saints Church. Bless the hands that knitted this prayer shawl, and bless Eugenia for all she does for God's kingdom. In Christ's name, Amen."

Mrs. Tyson pulled the prayer shawl up over her chest and clasped it with both shaking hands.

"We do appreciate so much all you do for the church," the Rev. Henderson said softly to her. He pressed his hand to her cheek and bent over her with a hug and a peck on her forehead.

The housekeeper appeared with a small tray bearing pills and a glass of water.

"I'll see you next week, Mrs. Tyson."

She smiled with grateful, misty eyes at her favorite parish priest. She squeezed his hand before letting him go.

As Will Henderson let himself out the big oak door, he stopped to reflect on the future of his parish. This woman had kept the church going for the last several years. Lord knows what would happen when she was gone.

He said his own prayer of thanks for the unknown woman – most likely a woman - who had knitted such a beautiful prayer shawl. Whoever she was, he thanked God that she had brought happiness to a generous old woman, if only for a moment.

Clarissa

A couple of months after I started donating my knitting to the church, I left a note tucked into the folds of a donated prayer shawl, suggesting that the women's shelter where I worked could use some of the shawls for the women housed there. I didn't hear anything for about two months. I told myself the note had gotten lost or more likely ignored and thrown away. I thought about retaliating by just giving my knitting to the clients myself, instead of throwing it in a donation box to go God knows where.

But one day, a grey-haired woman wearing a lovely silk dress showed up, out of the blue, with an armload of prayer shawls to donate. I said all the right things over the colorful shawls, many of them in shades of pink and other cheerful colors. I thanked her profusely and avoided asking how the woman thought to bring the shawls here. I certainly didn't let on that I suggested the donation myself.

From then on, about every two months or so, a nicely dressed woman appeared at the shelter – always a different lady, always in the middle of the day – with another stack of prayer shawls. As soon as I had the shawls to myself, I always took a peek to see if my own work had come back to me, so to speak.

But my own shawls never made it back to the women's shelter. I found that comforting in an odd sort of way – other women knitted shawls to support my clients, the women I cared a little too much about. Then my own work supported someone else who needed it, surely as much as the women fleeing nasty boyfriends and abusive husbands, often with a couple of little kids in tow.

As I dropped my latest two shawls in the donation box at the church and turned down the hall to my meeting, I tried to picture who would get the blue and grey shawl with the silver thread carefully embroidered in the shapes of doves. Maybe someone with cancer, maybe a woman in a nursing home with no one to visit or be with her at the end of her life. Maybe one of the ladies who delivered the shawls to the shelter would also take one of my shawls to a woman in great pain, and the woman would wrap it around her and feel like somebody cared.

Maybe an addict, somebody just like me, would get the triangular shawl knit in five shades of purple, with delicate lacing on the sides. Somebody trying to stay clean just for one day, then starting all over again the next day, would see the shawl as proof that she wasn't alone in this struggle. Somebody would wrap that shawl around her and find strength from somebody else who had gone through the same thing and survived, getting through one day at a time, just like you knitted one row at a time until finally, you got to where you always planned to be.

I pictured a young girl just getting off the streets or out of jail, perhaps – receiving the purple hued shawl and weeping, from frustration and from joy and from how hard she would have to work to wrestle her demons and keep them at bay.

As I made my way through the hallways of the church to my meeting, I realized I had a spring in my step. These meetings no longer filled me with a sense of dread at facing my demons. I actually looked forward to them.

All the knitting helped. Every time I got a craving for something I thought I needed, I reached for the knitting needles and whatever project I had going, and within a few minutes, the cravings passed.

I took my seat in the meeting. "I'm Clarissa, and I'm a substance abuser."

Cat Bed

"Stop it, Felicity!" Olivia batted the cat away from her laptop, and the feline sprang across the makeshift desk, straight onto the windowsill and out onto the roof. Oliva hoped her cat wouldn't run off too far or into the street. She had a blog post for a new client to finish and post within the next few minutes. With a tweet, Facebook post, and fifteen other platforms to cover, the last thing Olivia needed was a tabby cat stepping on the keys and destroying the last hour's work.

Okay, post finished. Quick proofing. Edit a few lines. Cut that sentence. Make that last point crystal clear and give it some zing. There. Finished. Auto-linked to most platforms. Rats, this one needs a sign-in and an update to the account. Remember the password, sign in, update, done. That one posted, too. Wait a few minutes, take a deep breath before checking the stats to make sure it's making the rounds.

Now, where had Felicity gone off to? Olivia got up to stretch. A cool breeze blew through her attic room in the hundred-year-old house near campus. Gazing out the window to the street below, she noticed several students making their way to class, bundled up in jackets and knitted hats. Turning away, Olivia almost wished she was still in school instead of trying to make a go of her own social media service. School had felt more secure, and she could usually find something cheap but healthy in one of the university cafeterias.

At least her rent was still low. She had moved into the top floor of the old Victorian-era house a year ago, saving hundreds of dollars a month off the amount she'd borrowed to pay for a shared dorm room and the university meal plan her mom thought she had to have. Before that, she had lived in a small house near the church where her mom worked as the housekeeper. Olivia had never felt at home there. Her mother still spoke Spanish at home, while Olivia had majored in English literature and creative writing. Olivia wanted her own home, on her own terms, not some charity house provided to a housekeeper and cleaner.

Olivia decided to tackle some cleaning of her own before she checked stats on her latest blog post. Even though she had vowed long ago to never work as a housekeeper like her mom, she still appreciated a tidy home. She fluffed the throw pillows she had found for fifty cents a piece at the church's charity store next to the food pantry, shaking her head at how wealthy people simply gave away expensive household goods. The pops of bright colors gave the dreary old attic room a little zest. And they matched her bright ceramic plates she had gotten at a flea market when she moved into this place. Looking around, she felt proud of herself, making an attractive and lively looking home out of throwaways and giveaways.

Which is why she didn't like that awful black, grey, and cream-colored blanket her mother had foisted on her. Apparently, her mom's boss, the priest at that church, had given it to her mom as some sort of symbol of prayers or good wishes or something. In any case, her mom insisted she take it home after their usual Sunday dinner last week. Even though it didn't match her place at all. Even though what Olivia needed was more steady clients willing to pay regularly for social media help, not just prayers and good wishes. Olivia had thrown it into the laundry basket next to the old bathtub and forgotten it. As she wiped down the sink and toilet of what she called her "bathroom corner," Olivia decided to try to trade the ugly blanket for something more useful the next time she and the girls downstairs got together to trade off clothes and books.

With her living spaces tidy, Olivia turned to her "home office corner," an antique writing table she had found abandoned across the street, along with a plank of wood positioned across two stacks of bricks she used for a printer stand and office supplies. Her office area looked like a wind storm had hit it – scraps of notes, a couple of files scattered across the floor, a journal, and various notebooks she used to keep track of blog post ideas stacked precariously beside the desk. At least Felicity hadn't knocked those down on top of the keyboard as she pushed herself off onto the window sill.

Olivia wondered where Felicity had gone. Looking out the window, she reassured herself that Felicity was not lying dead in the middle of the street. She called Felicity's name and turned around towards the bathroom corner, surprised to hear a "meow" from across the room. Following the sound, she found her cat curled up in the laundry basket, on top of the ugly brown and black prayer shawl. The cat must have snuck back through the window while she had cleaned up her office area, and the colors of the prayer shawl camouflaged Felicity's brown and black tabby fur to perfection.

"Come here, you." Olivia scooped up the cat and the ugly blanket in one swoop and hugged the cat, swaddled in the prayer shawl like a baby. As much as Olivia disliked the colors of the prayer shawl, it felt soft and cuddly. Felicity purred.

"So you've got your own prayer shawl, huh Felicity?" She stroked the cat's long, purring midsection. Felicity closed her eyes and soaked up the love.

"I guess everybody needs prayers." Olivia checked her watch. She'd need to look at stats on the blog post pretty soon. She settled Felicity and the prayer shawl back in the laundry basket. The cat got up, turned a couple of circles, and resumed her nap.

At least she wasn't on top of my keyboard, Olivia thought. That answered a prayer for sure.

Olivia opened the stats page and frowned at the low response to the blog post. Oh well, she thought. Maybe stats would pick up later in the afternoon. She looked over at Felicity on her new cat bed. She hoped – maybe even prayed – people out there in the cyber-sphere would find her writing, the writing she worked so hard on…and click that "like" button.

Olivia forgot about her blog for a moment. She brushed her long, dark hair behind her back and started a new blog post, one she hoped a new client would like enough to pay her on a weekly basis.

As she typed, she wondered if she dared tell her mother she had turned the prayer shawl into a cat bed.

Domestic Violence Shelter

Franny picked up her knitting needles and settled in for a long morning of knitting in the sun room of her home. The house was clean, the laundry started, and she had no appointments on the calendar. So Franny could knit most of the day, if she wanted.

She had retired early, having spent too many long hours, early mornings, and more than a few weekends working as an administrative assistant for a big law firm downtown. Her husband still worked, so she spent most days alone.

Frankly, she was bored. She missed what used to seem like mindless gossip with the other women she worked with. As she knitted, Franny told herself to move on. She now had the comfort and security of never having to put up with a stress-ridden job or abusive boss, ever again.

Shortly after she retired, one of the ladies who always attended the Sunday service at their church, dressed to the nines – one of the *"grande dames"* as Franny's husband called them – offered to show Franny how to knit prayer shawls. Franny worked under the tutelage of Melba Strickland, a woman with white hair, a pastel colored suit, and southern drawl. They met together several times after the Sunday worship service, knitting in the back pew while the cleaning lady worked around them. After a month of lessons and practice, Franny could knit about as well as her teacher. Finally, Melba had deemed Franny ready to handle the task of knitting all by herself.

Franny wrapped the almost-finished fluffy pink prayer shawl around her knees while she worked on the last couple of inches of her project. She knitted, making blocks of stockinette stitch with a yarn-over lace row every fourteen stitches, for a solid hour and a half before getting up to stretch and use the bathroom. She made herself a cup of tea, turned on the TV news, and resumed her project.

She planned to donate this particular shawl to a women's shelter downtown. Franny had purchased fluffy, pink yarn for the project and made the prayer shawl large enough to completely envelope a woman her own size, remembering the priest's suggestion to "love generously, knit generously" when making items to give to those in need.

Franny finished her pink fuzzy prayer shawl, tied up loose ends, and folded the shawl neatly into a rectangle, putting it on a special shelf in her craft room until she could drive it over to the church for donation. She still had two hours until she needed to start dinner, so she slipped into bed for a power nap. As she let the luxurious cotton sheets fall around her body, she reminded herself how profoundly blessed she was to be able to take a nap in the middle of the afternoon.

Tonya

"I want THAT one!" I made a grab for the pink fuzzy blanket that woman had just brought in. I spied that thing in amongst the pile, and I knowed it was mine.

"Damn, Tonya, let somebody else get one'a them things," the girl who bunked in my room said behind my back. Not that I cared. I wanted that pink one. It spoke to me.

The director had come in that morning and said somebody from a church planned to bring in somethin' called "prayer shawls" to hand out to us.

I didn't have a prayer of gettin' outta this mess I was in, but I never passed on a freebie. Two days had passed since I had come here, Keesha and Josh in tow and their ears hurtin' and snot runnin' down their faces. I'd had enough, and Darrell needed to find that out.

"This is my flag," I told her and everybody else. "This is my girl power flag." I held up that pink blanket with both arms and strutted around that whole room like I was some-body.

"Girl power, that's a crock," one of the old gals muttered under her breath. I laughed. I knowed there weren't no girl power in the place. Ever' one of us had a black eye, an ugly old yellow bruise, somethin' we didn't talk much about.

"Tonya, gib me that blanket. I gib you this yella 'un.'"

"Hell no. This one's mine." I folded the thing up and took it back to my room. The kids had started to wake up, so I acted real quiet so I'd get just a minute to myself.

I took that big ole pink blanket, and I hung it acrost the front of my bunk like a big old flag. This is me, I wanted to tell ever-body. This is mine.

I washed my face off and decided to take a little snooze before the kids got up and started botherin' me. But no, somebody was a tappin' on the door.

"Damnation," I said. "Yes?"

That director woman stood at the door. "Tonya? I've got some possibilities for you to look at."

I let her in. She kept a talkin' without a thought to the kids sleepin' in the bunks.

"We've got a job for you – downtown – bussing tables and cleaning up at one of the new restaurants. You can start as early as this afternoon."

I heard the kids a moanin' from up top. I stood on tippy toe and saw Keesha and Josh pushin' each other and squabblin' up in the top bunk. "What about the kids?" I asked.

The director woman, Clarice or Clarissa or something, looked up at the top bunk. She flipped her blond, messy-lookin' hair over her shoulder and peeped over the bunk railing. Josh sat up, and she smiled at him. "We can give you a voucher for day care. In the meantime, they're welcome to stay here."

I considered my options. I could go back home, where there'd be hell to pay for sure. I could take it. I prided myself on that. One more black eye, and Darrell'd be sorry for it. I could promise him that.

Or I could get out of this glorified kindy-garten and make some money. "I'll take it."

The director woman nodded. We all knew she liked it when one of the girls went back to work. "Come on, kids, let's get you some breakfast."

The kids crawled out from under the covers on the top bunk and went off with Clarice or whatever her name was. I threw my stuff into my bag and looked around to make sure I hadn't left nothin.' If my luck held, I'd get a voucher for one of them apartments on the other side of downtown, at least for the time being. We'd be outta here soon.

Just in case, I pulled down my big pink blanket and stuffed it in my bag. Half of it hung out the top, but I didn't care none. I liked it.

I took one last look at the room we'd shacked up in for two days, and I headed out to my new job. I hoped the work wouldn't be too nasty.

Franny finished her latest prayer shawl and tossed it on the growing stack of finished knitting ready for donation. She climbed the stairs to her dressing room and took a good five minutes brushing her dyed blond hair. She could use a touch-up next week, she decided. It would give her something to do.

She heard the door open and close again downstairs. Robert must have come home for lunch. She had cleaned up the kitchen right after breakfast. She hoped he would notice.

"What are you doing home?" she asked him. He had both a messenger bag slung over his shoulder and a brief case in hand. He stood in the light of the two-story foyer of the house, not moving, not saying anything.

"Robert? What's wrong?"

Robert dropped the briefcase to the floor and let the messenger bag slip off his shoulder. He slumped over to the bar on the far side of the living room and poured himself a Scotch. After three deep sips, he poured himself another.

Franny took a seat on one of the peach-colored sofas, silently waiting for him to say something.

Robert moved to in front of the picture window overlooking the riverbank in the distance. "The firm let me go," he said bitterly.

"Oh no."

"Oh yes." He finished the rest of his second drink. "And how am I supposed to get a new job at my age?"

Franny let a tiny smile slip onto her face. She had enjoyed the long days of nothing to do but knit all day. But now, she could go back to work.

As Franny packed her tote bag for her first day back at her old law firm, she included a skein of yarn and a pair of knitting needles. After two hours of answering client's emails and phone calls, she took out her needles and knitted a couple of rows. After ten minutes, she was ready to tackle the rest of the morning.

Franny went with the other women in her office to the new café that had recently opened a few blocks from the law firm. Franny tucked her purse under the table, knitting needles poking out. The young waitress glanced at them before pulling out her order pad.

Her name tag read, "Tonya."

"What canna I get for ya today, ladies?"

Weekly Therapy Session

Melba Strickland arrived early for her regular Friday morning Knitting Guild meeting. She wanted everything just so – lights on in the church parlor, chairs arranged in a tight circle (better for conversation), coffee brewed and a box of butter cookies put out.

Since 1969, Melba had taken on the duties of arriving first and making sure everything at church ran smoothly. She and her late husband had joined the church as newlyweds, grown into young marrieds with children as the fledging mission church had grown into a full-fledged parish, then settled into the empty-nested widowhood of her later years as the church needed more and more maintenance, both within and without. Melba had become the first woman to serve as a vestry leader in the congregation, and she had gotten there by taking care of details. She had no reason to stop now.

Minutes later, her old friend Martha Craig limped in, wearing sweat pants and an oversized sweatshirt. She tossed her knitting tote bag on the floor in front of her preferred seat and flopped herself down, groaning in arthritic pain.

"You're not playing the part of saintly Anglican nun today?" Melba drawled at her, taking a long and critical look at her friend's sweat suit. Ten years ago, Martha had gotten herself ordained a deacon. She had – in Melba's opinion – overdone the thing by calling herself "Sister Martha" and wearing a long white robe when she attended church functions.

"I'm tired," Martha said.

Melba settled into her own preferred seat at the head of the circle and pulled out a skein of yarn – in fire engine red – and a pair of big chunky knitting needles. She knitted a couple of rows onto a small rectangle of knitting before binding off the project and tossing it over onto a stack of big knitting squares stacked on the sofa of the church parlor.

"Isn't that a little small for a prayer shawl?" Martha asked.

Melba smirked. "It has come to my attention that our prayer shawls have, on occasion, become cat beds."

Martha frowned. "How's that?"

"Father Henderson gave one of the prayer shawls to Cassandra. He said she's all concerned about her daughter, thinking she won't find a decent job. Father Henderson says really, the daughter works at home all the time on one of those social media things – I don't know really understand it. He says he thinks Cassandra's really upset, thinkin' she might have to go back to Honduras. But anyway, he gave her one of the prayer shawls, thinkin' it would help her feel more secure – that the church cares about her and all – and the next thing he knew, Cassandra came to him all cryin' and what-not, saying her daughter had given her prayer shawl to the cat!"

Martha chuckled. "Well, cats are people, too."

"I suppose so," Melba responded. "In any case, one of the new members who just moved to town went to Father Henderson that same afternoon, asking if we could help with the animal shelter over on Kingston

Pike. It seems they need soft, fuzzy blankets for the cats."

"So here we are," Martha said.

"Here we are. Knitting cat blankets."

Martha shook her head. "It's not like we don't have anything else going on here." She pulled her own knitting needles out of her tote bag and resumed work on a long piece of navy-blue knitting. "Did somebody take a prayer shawl over to Roger Livingstone?" she asked after several rows.

Melba thought for a moment. "Yes. I think that fuzzy purple one Ginger knitted went to him last week."

"Good. Purple will make the old guy happy. He always did want to be a bishop. Never made it."

Martha knitted in silence, lost in thought. After another row on her long piece of knitting, she suddenly put her needles down in her lap. "I can't do this anymore. It's too much. It's too much for anybody."

Melba stopped her knitting mid-row. These group knitting sessions had, on more than one occasion, turned into much-needed therapy sessions. "Can't do what? Knitting?"

Martha shook her head. "No. The knitting actually helps. I mean all this church stuff. Father Roger handled a lot of the nursing home visits for us, even though he's officially retired. And he's out of commission now. Probably for good, if you want to know the truth. And the rest of the clergy are busy with meetings and all the paperwork, fundraising, writing sermons – all that stuff. Which leaves me for the hospital visits. And it's too much."

Melba resumed her knitting, taking her time before responding. Sometimes people just needed to vent; they didn't necessarily need a response. "What makes you think you have to do it all? What makes you think the clergy have to do it all, for that matter?"

Martha took a deep breath and picked up her knitting needles again, jabbing them into the yarn. "You're right. You're absolutely right."

"Don't y'all preach something about all the rest of us working as the hands and feet of Christ?"

"We do."

"Then give it up," Melba told her.

"Some days, I'd like to give it all up."

"That's okay."

"I mean not do more than anybody else in the congregation."

"You've already given up that white robe you took to wearing."

"I haven't given it up," Martha sharply replied. "I just felt like wearing sweat pants today."

Melba concentrated on her knitting. "Uh-huh. Sounds like maybe it's time to give all that stuff up for good. Let other people step up and do the work of the church."

At that moment, Ginger Jordan appeared at the doorway of the church parlor, a cheerful polka dotted knitting bag in tow. "Sorry I'm late – I had to finish up some accounting work for the food pantry." The young woman lit up the room with her smile.

Melba patted a seat beside her. "Come sit. Take a break from the food pantry."

As Ginger got settled, Melba turned her attention back to Martha. "I mean it. You might need to give some things up. Death and resurrection, remember? Give it up before you have renewed life."

"I'll think about it," Martha grumbled.

"Something wrong?" Ginger asked.

"Nah, we're just complainin' about church work, is all," Melba replied.

"Something I could help with?"

"How do you feel about cat beds?" Melba laughed.

Mother's Day

Abby

"Abby, Melba left the prayer shawls you blessed yesterday in your office," the church secretary called to me as I headed to the oversized closet I called my office.

"Thanks," I called back. I could use prayers myself. I had just left the rector's office, frustrated, depressed, and disillusioned. And now I had to go coddle someone who had a meltdown over my Sunday sermon. I would have to defend the very crux of my ministry against a presumably spoiled woman who had practically everything a human being could ever want.

I didn't want to do this. I knew I had to do this.

It all began when my boss, Will Henderson, assigned the Mother's Day sermon to me. On top of that, he asked me to lead the blessing of the new prayer shawls the knitting guild had made for all new mothers in the parish.

I suspected he asked me to handle these duties only because I'm a woman and should, therefore, lead all things related to feminine pursuits. Even though I wasn't a mother myself, had no plans for motherhood, and had proven myself doing hard-core relief and development work. Meanwhile, my male supervisor assigned himself the world hunger day sermon. I knew sexism lurked within the church hierarchy, and usually, I simply gritted my teeth and did my job. But I didn't like what I saw as stereotyping on the rector's part, not at all.

For not the first time, I had thoughts of huge regret in taking on parish ministry. These thoughts were always there, ever since I had put on a skirted suit and a clerical collar, relegating my old khaki shorts, filthy tennis shoes, and t-shirt collection to the garbage bin. But I needed this experience to move up the clerical hierarchy. I knew this. My bishop had repeatedly told me so. So here I was. I'd come up with a sermon and meaningful, heart-warming things to say for the Mother's Day extravaganza at All Saints Episcopal Church, despite not having a clue of what it meant to be a mother.

Blessings. That was the theme of the day. After two days of prayer and – quite honestly – personal soul searching, I focused on how every one of us is a blessing. All mothers, all children, everyone in the village that was All Saints who contributed to raising up the next generation of children, the next generation of Christianity.

I could build on this theme later to lead my parish in seeing children in developing nations as blessings, too. But I had to start here. I had to start by asking my parishioners to see the children in their own parish as tremendous blessings – plus themselves and each of their own efforts to give to those in less powerful, more vulnerable positions in this society.

I preached it. They got it. I could see it. You get this feeling when the congregation is with you, when they really hear you, when you get them to a new place in their thinking and in their spiritual growth. That's what it's all about. And I had done that, I knew it deep in my own soul.

Coming down from the pulpit, I felt the power of the Holy Spirit within me. I called for the Knitting Guild to come to the altar, and I placed my hands in blessing on every one of the prayer shawls they had knitted for the new mothers in the parish. I prayed in thanksgiving for each of their efforts, all of their time and prayer as they knitted these prayer shawls, and for the blessing of the new mothers and precious children with whom we would wrap the prayers of our entire parish community.

After the service, several parishioners remarked on how powerful the sermon and the blessing had been. I took no credit for the words that had merely passed through me. But I felt I had grown over the course of that week. I could do this. I could serve as a parish priest and make a difference in the lives of these people.

Then all hell broke loose.

"Abigail, I need to see you about something," Will Henderson's voice came through the phone line while I worked in my office the following Monday morning.

"I'll be right there." I didn't like the sound of Will's tone of voice. The rector kept a close eye on every little thing that went on in the parish. That was his job, he told me when I joined the staff. If somebody gets upset or doesn't like something we're doing, they quit coming. They drop their pledge. And pledges are what keep this whole ship afloat, he had told me. I sighed and walked down the hall to his office.

"We have a problem," the rector snapped as soon as I crossed the threshold.

I reached to close the door behind me.

"Not necessary," Will said. "This won't take long."

I took a seat in the wing-backed arm chair beside the door. Just when I thought I had started fitting in, I'd done something or said something that, unknowingly, had rubbed somebody the wrong way. I couldn't win.

"Mrs. Tyson just called...."

I wanted to groan. Mrs. Tyson was the church's largest donor, by far. Whatever Mrs. Tyson wanted, Mrs. Tyson got. I questioned the theology of this approach.

"You need to take one of those prayer shawls over to Tabitha Terrell this morning. Before lunch. No delay."

I nodded. "Yes Sir."

"Tabitha's been trying to get pregnant for the last year and a half. She had one of those in vitro procedures last month, and she found right before Mother's Day that it hadn't worked. Mrs. Tyson said she was devastated by your sermon. She thinks she's somehow cursed...not worthy of motherhood. In any case, she needs to know she is as 'blessed' as the rest of the women in the parish."

"I see." I honestly hadn't thought about women who might not be able to get pregnant.

Personally, I was more concerned with avoiding pregnancy.

"You have some serious pastoral care back-peddling to do."

"And this is Mrs. Tyson's concern, because...?"

Will grimaced at what he took as a rude remark.

"Tabitha is her grandniece. She is Mrs. Tyson's only surviving relative and likely her heir. You should know this."

I nodded. There was so much I was expected to know but couldn't fathom how I was to learn.

"Since Mrs. Tyson doesn't have children, I think we might assume she struggled with infertility herself. It's a sore spot for her, I'm sure."

"I'll get over there now."

Grabbing one of the prayer shawls Melba had just left in my office, I pulled on my suit jacket and headed out.

"I'll be out for an hour or so," I called to the church secretary. Gripping my car keys, I headed out to see Tabitha Terrell.

Tabitha Terrell's house was an old 1930's era brick cottage with a slate roof. It sat on the edge of one of the better neighborhoods in town. A Beemer was parked in the drive, and rows of pink azaleas lined the front walkway. It didn't look like a place where the inhabitants would be in any kind of distress at all.

Clutching the pale green prayer shawl like a security blanket, I prayed for words of grace to share with this woman, along with the courage to own up to my failure to even think about women who couldn't have children.

The door opened, and a white Westie dog immediately jumped up against my knees to greet me. Tabitha tried to pull him down. She wore a pair of black yoga pants and a sleeveless athletic shirt. Her short dark hair looked ruffled, and she wore no make-up. From the puffiness of her face, she looked like she had recently had a good cry.

"I'm so sorry. He's too friendly sometimes." Tabitha averted my eyes, reaching down to pull the dog back inside her home.

"No worries," I said. Behind Tabitha, I could spy a living room filled with comfortable chintz-upholstered chairs and a Persian rug. A baby grand piano sat in the corner, and soft floor lamps made the dark room look cozy - but a little sad, too.

How the heck should I start this conversation? "I'm Abigail Mills. I'm a priest at All Saints Church. I hear you've had some bad news....?"

Tabitha grimaced slightly and rolled her eyes. "I can't believe my aunt called the church about that."

I took a deep breath. So I had to deal with a breach of confidence here as well. "I'm so sorry. I don't think Father Henderson realized that was confidential information. Mrs. Tyson asked for a pastoral visit...."

"Listen, I only go to church because my aunt wants to go, and I'm the only family she has. I take her there because she lays a guilt trip on me otherwise."

"I understand," I said. "We just got the phone call from Mrs. Tyson, saying you were very upset by the sermon I preached yesterday. I only wanted people to see all children as blessed. I assure you, I didn't mean that women with infertility issues weren't blessed."

Tabitha looked away. "I just don't want to talk about it, that's all."

"I understand. Our mistake. Father Henderson asked me to come over and bring you a prayer shawl right away…to make sure you knew you are blessed, too. We all are."

As I held the pale green prayer shawl out to her, the dog pushed in front of her to take a good, long sniff of the delicately crocheted hem of the prayer shawl.

"Max, get down," Tabitha scolded. "I'm so sorry. I'm being really rude. Would you like to come in? At least for a cup of coffee, maybe?"

The dog looked up at me with a friendly tongue hanging out his mouth and shiny dark brown eyes. Tabitha opened the door wider and motioned for me to enter.

She left me in the living room with the dog for a good fifteen minutes while she made coffee. When she returned, handing me a steaming ceramic mug, she began speaking before she even sat down.

"Listen, I'm cried out. I'm done. This is the third time I've been through in vitro fertilization, and I'm not going through it again. I'm ready to move on." She plopped down on a sofa facing me.

"Sounds like you've started the healing process," I said. "That usually doesn't begin until you hit rock bottom."

Tabitha looked me straight in the eye. "That's not what I expected you to say."

I put my coffee mug down on the table in front of me. "We all get to the point where we can't go on with a bad situation. Clearly, you've gotten to that point, and you're ready to move on. That's a huge step forward."

"You think so?" Tabitha looked down at her coffee mug.

"Yes. Absolutely."

"Infertility sucks. I mean, look at all the women in the world who have too many children or don't want children at all. Look at all the awful parents who beat their kids or just plain don't pay any attention to them. Nick and I just want to give a great home to a new little person. And here we are. Nothing happens."

"You're right," I told her. "None of it's fair. When I worked in sub-Saharan Africa, I saw all these women whose kids died of malaria as toddlers. Then they'd have another kid, and that kid would die, too. And then there's the families who can't feed their children."

"So you're not here to tell me I'm damned to hell and rendered infertile because I'm an awful person?" Tabitha asked.

At that moment, the Westie jumped up into Tabitha's lap and made himself at home. "Your dog seems to think you're an okay person," I told her.

Tabitha winced, tears began falling down her cheeks. "I needed to hear that. I feel so demoralized. This infertility stuff has worn me down."

I slid over to the sofa. "I'm going to pray with you," I said. I put my hands on her shoulders and prayed silently for several moments. I prayed that she would become a mother. I prayed that she would find a child, and that a child would find her. I prayed for the Holy Spirit to fully heal her and her husband and bring redemption out of their pain. Then I made the sign of the cross on her forehead.

"Thank you," Tabitha said in barely a whisper. She wiped the tears off her face. "Sorry, I thought I was over this."

"You will be," I told her with full assurance, "but it will take time." The dog looked up at me, wagging its shaggy white tail like a cheerful flag of surrender.

As I prepared to leave, I remembered the pale green prayer shawl I had tossed over a chair when I entered the house. "Oh, I brought you this. It's a prayer shawl. It's something we give out to anyone who needs healing – of any kind."

"I thought the church just gave those to new mothers," Tabitha said.

"Nope. They go to anyone who needs extra prayer. You qualify."

"I wish I didn't."

"Believe me," I said, "once you're getting up in four in the morning to feed a baby and change shitty diapers, you'll really need extra prayers. I hear it's brutal."

Tabitha cracked a smile for the first time during my visit. "Don't tell me that!"

"Be careful of what you ask of God," I replied.

As I pulled out of the driveway, Tabitha watched me leave, the pale green prayer shawl clutched in her hands. The dog watched me as well, tail wagging and tongue hanging out.

Six months later, I got a phone call from Tabitha. "We're going to adopt!" she announced as soon as I said hello. "We leave to meet our little boy next week."

"That's wonderful," I told her. "You'll be a great mom."

"Ruff!" her dog barked in agreement.

Going Home

"Ouch this hurts." The whole left side of Samantha's leg roared with pain seconds into her first stretch. She cringed, her leg propped up on two vegetable crates pilfered from the corner market. Worse yet, the claustrophobia of her miniscule New York City apartment closed in on her soul. Between the constant traffic noises and the lack of fresh air, she struggled to calm down enough to relax into the stretch she knew she had to do.

The doctor had diagnosed iliotibial syndrome, overuse of the muscle that ran from hip to knee. Pain radiated all the way down to her ankle, and the doctor had grounded her from rehearsals with the corps de ballet she had worked so hard to join. If she didn't cease and desist from all the jumps, turns, and anything else requiring outer thigh muscles (which amounted to the company's entire repertoire), her professional dance career would end at age twenty-four.

In the meantime, the physical therapist had ordered stretches of at least thirty minutes a day, three times a day. Samantha pled her case for simple exercises at the barre, working on low plies and battements, but the therapist said no.

"You need to stretch. Period," she had barked at the tall, overly thin ballerina.

After a full five minutes of simply stretching her leg out straight in front of herself while sitting on a rickety kitchen chair, Samantha resigned herself to dropping to the floor and onto her ancient, pitted yoga mat, surrounded by dust bunnies. She had talked the therapist into letting her do sit-ups to keep her core toned. Tired of someone else calling the shots on her own body, she also slipped in some yoga stretches for her spine. Surely that couldn't hurt.

Time for the most important stretch, the stretch of her hip and upper thigh. Samantha flipped herself upright on the yoga mat, crossed her left leg in front of herself and slid her right leg to the back, flat to the floor.

"Owwwwww." Her left leg tingled like it was stuck in an electrical socket. That meant the stretch worked, but damn it hurt.

Samantha wondered if all the stretches would be worth the effort. She had achieved her dream of dancing in a NYC dance company, sure. But all she had gotten out of it otherwise was an overpriced, poor excuse for a living space and long hours in the studio. Her friends back home assumed she spent long afternoons jogging through Central Park, shopping at hipster stores, and taking in all the museums and galleries. But the truth was, she didn't have time for any leisurely strolls through parks or galleries and couldn't afford most of the clothes.

Maybe she should chuck it all and go back home, she thought for not the first time. The one time she had taken a long walk through Central Park, it reminded her of the parklike neighborhood she grew up in. Trees and wildflowers everywhere, birds chirping, and plenty of warmth most of the year round. Why had she wanted to move to a huge city with constant gridlock and the only greenery found at those corner flower shops she also couldn't afford to shop in?

Samantha sighed, telling herself you can't go home again, not really. Her childhood home might give her a more peaceful existence, but she wouldn't get to dance professionally. Of course, if she didn't get back in tip-top shape, she wouldn't dance professionally again anyway. As she braced herself to faceplant herself into the yoga mat again, she looked around for something, anything, to slip under her head to keep the dust out of her nose. She needed a pillow…or something…while she held the stretch that might save her career.

Samantha crawled the short length of her apartment to grab a package she had tossed next to her small sofa bed, the only substantial piece of furniture she owned. She remembered her mom had sent a squishy, pillow-sized parcel a week or so ago, about the time the pain in her leg became constant. She'd called her mom in tears, pouring out her fears and tears to her mother in a way she could do with no one here in the City. She imagined her mother seated cross-legged on the large white sofa of her spacious childhood home, gazing out the window to the forest of oaks and maples behind the house. Her mom convinced her to go to a doctor. "It might be something easily fixed," she had advised. "And let me know sweetie, as soon as you hear something."

Several days later, the package arrived in the mail, with a return address from the church her mom attended, the church where Samantha had gone to Sunday School back in the days when she simply took ballet lessons twice a week, back before dance became a full-time job. When Samantha called her mom to tell her what the doctor had diagnosed, her mom told her she had added Samantha's name to the church prayer list. One of the Knitting Guild members her mom had known for years had also offered to send a prayer shawl to her.

Samantha had eye-rolled and tossed the package aside when it arrived. What was it supposed to do, magically make her pain go away?

But a nice, hand-knitted shawl would be just the thing to prop under her chin while stretching three times a day. She ripped open the package and smiled to find a fluffy pile of pink, red, and purple yarn, hand-knitted into a small blanket. She shook it out and refolded it into a fat, round cylinder.

Samantha slid her legs back into position, finally relaxing into the stretch. Her head dropped onto the rolled-up prayer shawl. She quit thinking. She quit worrying.

After five whole minutes of silence, she switched to the other side and dropped into a state of meditation, her head melting into the prayer shawl. Taking in a long breath, she caught the faint smell of perfume, an old brand, something a woman of another generation might wear.

Switching back to her sore left side, Samantha leaned her nose firmly into the prayer shawl. She felt like a child again, pressing her face into her mother's shoulder, smelling her Chanel No. 5 wafting down from behind her ears. She almost fell asleep.

After a good thirty-minute stretch, Samantha raised herself up into down-dog pose, then into an upright mountain pose. She gasped. Her left leg didn't hurt. And for the first time in several weeks!

The rolled-up prayer shawl, now tied up into a long roll with a piece of pale pink ribbon from a favorite pair of pointe shoes, became part of her regular exercise equipment. She filled up her laundry basket with a stretch band, a small rubber ball, a couple of yoga blocks, and the prayer shawl. She shuddered to think what the woman who had knitted this prayer shawl would think if she knew it had become therapy equipment, but it worked. Nothing else had just the right softness and depth to both hold up her head and make her feel so relaxed in the process.

After two weeks of using the prayer shawl for her thrice daily stretches, Samantha felt better – and not just physically. The guy at the deli down the street told her it was nice to see a smile on her face for a change. The stack of bills she feared she couldn't pay if she couldn't dance didn't freak her out quite so much. She slept better at night.

Then Samantha started hearing something like voices as she eased into the deep stretch that made fresh oxygen and blood flow into her leg. "You don't have to do this," she could almost hear someone whisper. "You don't have to wear out your body so much."

The whispers lurked in Samantha's brain, asking her how dedicated she really was to dance. They questioned whether she really wanted to live in New York. They even suggested that she could dance just for fun, and back home to boot. She caught herself glancing at the employment ads in the newspaper she found in the subway on the way to therapy sessions. She found herself asking her physical therapist how she came to be a therapist, and why.

Stretching sessions morphed into soul-searching sessions. During preliminary stretches, sitting on a chair with her leg flexed out and held up by a long flexy stretch band, her mind opened a door that normally remained closed. As she shifted into deeper stretches on the floor, she eased into her own private therapy room for some difficult internal discussions.

By the time her head hit the prayer shawl during the deepest stretches, there was no more pretending. No more agendas. No more fooling herself about what she really wanted from life. "Let it all go," the whispers said.

Samantha's leg healed. But by the time the therapist had cleared her to dance again, she had packed up almost everything in the tiny apartment, ready to ship it all back home.

"I don't want to dance again," she told her physical therapist. "At least not on stage, and not all the time. Dance gave my life a structure, a purpose, a goal. But there has to be more to life. Surely there's other jobs I could do that won't wear out my body before I'm twenty-five."

Before she headed to LaGuardia for her flight home, she took one last look around what she once fantasized as the dancer's apartment of dreams. Once a symbol of late teen independence in the city, the place now felt as cramped and confining as it really was. She had barely enough room to turn around, much less live a life.

The basket of therapy equipment sat on the floor, the last of her possessions not either packed up or given away. She had slept on her yoga mat the night before and didn't relish dragging it through the airport. So she simply left it behind. The stretch band folded up nicely in her purse. The yoga blocks would stay, no longer needed.

But the rolled-up prayer shawl, she just couldn't leave behind. She slipped off the pink toe shoe ribbon holding it into a cylinder and folded it into a more conventional small blanket. She tucked it into her big black dance bag and headed off to the airport.

"You're back!" Samantha's mom searched her eyes, trying to decipher whether her daughter felt crushed, disappointed, or maybe even relieved after giving up her dream of dancing with a New York City ballet company.

"Yep. I'm back. For good," Samantha told her mother. She smiled the smile of someone who had just taken a burden off her back. Surprisingly, to her mother, her lanky daughter had a fuzzy pink blanket draped over her shoulders.

"That's the prayer shawl Jenny Lawson made for you," her mom said. "I honestly didn't think you would even look at it."

Samantha unwrapped the shawl from her shoulders and tucked it back into her dance bag. "It may have saved my life."

Jenny Lawson plopped down on the only seat available at Gate 35, the gate where flights from Washington, D.C. took off every few minutes to smaller airports all over the country. After taking a few moments to catch her breath, she unzipped the outside pocket of her carry-on and pulled out her work-in-progress, a navy-blue wool scarf, basket-weave stitch.

Before she had finished a row, an elderly woman sitting across from her pulled her own knitting needles and red wool yarn out of her oversized purse and settled in for a nice long knitting session. The woman had white hair and elegant clothing, paired with sensible shoes and a walking cane propped next to her carry-on.

"Might as well join you," the elderly woman said.

Jenny looked up from her knitting. "What are you making?" she asked the older woman. It was the question everyone asked of a knitter, the widely acknowledged standard opening line for conversation that could, if the knitter chose, begin a long friendship or stall out at a simple word: scarf, blanket, socks.

"Well, I don't really know," the woman replied. "I started out making a sweater for one of my granddaughters, but I don't think I have enough yarn. So maybe a pillow case?"

"I understand," Jenny nodded. "I knit for therapy. If it turns out long enough for a scarf, all the better." She had just finished closing a deal that had taken two weeks to sort out, with umpteen delays and changes of terms she had to re-write into the closing documents on the fly and away from her office. She had spent more time in her hotel's "business center" than she ever wanted to spend again. She wanted to go home.

"We all do!" the woman replied. She continued with her project, knitting at a snail's pace. Jenny noticed that the woman didn't even look at her work as her gnarled fingers slipped the stitches from one needle to another.

Jenny preferred to look at each stitch as a means of blocking out the rest of the world. She had thrown in the towel on making anything more complicated than an oversized scarf. Having to count and fret over knitting projects made crafting a chore rather than an outlet for relaxation.

The two knitters continued on with their respective projects. The bond had been made. They would both work in companionable silence. No further attempts at talking would likely be made. And that was okay. Each of the women would occasionally look up and perhaps slip the other a slight smile, a small acknowledgement of something in common in the midst of the busiest waiting area in the airport.

All around them, travelers grabbed luggage and headed down the escalator to their flights. Others took their seats. A man on the end of the row of seats chowed down on a burger, the smell drifting over everyone in the vicinity. Two small children, a boy and a girl, played hide and seek under their parents' seats at the other end of the row.

In the wide hallway down the middle of the airport concourse, hordes of people pushed and pivoted to make their flights, dashed into restrooms, went in or out of the airport shops, or wearily emerged from the arrival gates and trudged towards the ground transportation signs. But Jenny and the woman sitting across from her at Gate 35 calmly knitted and purled, an enclave of peace and quiet amidst the hustle and bustle of National Airport.

Jenny pulled her scarf out to its full length to assess whether she should bind off or keep knitting. She decided a few more rows wouldn't hurt. It was the process, not the product, she valued.

Back in the hotel, she had gladly shut the door behind her each night and picked up her beloved size eight bamboo needles and yarn, glad to finally take a break from other people and the constant stress of closing a deal. If she could only pull out her needles and yarn at the closing table and knit a couple of rows every hour or so, what a difference that would make in lowering her blood pressure and general attitude.

But she couldn't. Professional woman didn't knit. Period. She had enough trouble with men – and even other women – taking her seriously as a lawyer. She wore all the right clothes – black pants and a tasteful silk blouse, moderately high-heeled pumps and an expensive blazer jacket – to make the point up front that she was somebody who should be listened to, acknowledged, respected. Pulling out a couple of "old lady" knitting needles and yarn would kill that carefully curated image faster than you could say "sex discrimination." Not fair, Jenny knew, but that's the way it was.

She glanced at the older woman slowly knitting her way through the red wool yarn. Her hands had the dark spots you often saw on very old people. The lines on her face and the white of her hair pegged her as being of a generation of woman who could knit in public and feel no shame whatsoever.

Jenny remembered her own mother, recently deceased, who had not pursued a career, with no ambitions beyond motherhood and a well-appointed home. Her mother didn't knit, but she often spent her mornings sewing in the little craft room on the second story of the family home, her own little enclave of peace and quiet, a place away from the cares of raising a family and of constantly catering to others' needs.

Jenny learned to knit in law school. During her terrifying, anxiety-fraught first year, she found herself biting her nails down to the quick and even pulling at the skin around her nails until they bled. When a classmate spied her hands and winced in disgust, Jenny realized she needed an outlet. She tried joining an aerobics class on campus, with mixed results. Exercise helped, but she needed something she could do whenever the overwhelming stress of law school got too much, something she could pick up and do on an as-needed basis.

So she wandered into a knitting store one Saturday and asked the sixty-year-old women running the place to teach her how to knit. The knitting store ladies eagerly and kindly set her up with a pair of size nine straight needles and a big ball of worsted weight yarn. Jenny chose a spring green color, thinking it would create cool, calm, non-threatening vibes to soothe her soul as she worked. Jenny learned to knit, purl, bind on, and bind off during one long afternoon session at the knit store. She never picked up the speed of the veteran knitters who taught her, but Jenny didn't want speed. She wanted to stop biting her nails.

After that one long session, Jenny rarely returned to the knit shop. All the regulars there were at least thirty years older than herself. She went for occasional help when she didn't understand a pattern or had gotten a project hopelessly messed up, but otherwise, knitting became a completely solitary activity. Her own means of checking out and leaving the real world for a few minutes…or hours.

Jenny jabbed at her knitting needles and thought about what her life might have been, if only she had not worked so hard, not fought so hard to make partner, had relaxed a little. She might had stayed married. She might have had kids. She might have a flabby midsection and not particularly cared.

"Well, that's my flight," the elderly woman across from her announced, perhaps to Jenny and perhaps to no one in particular.

"Have a good flight," Jenny responded, flashing the woman a smile.

The red wool yarn got shoved into a large leather tote bag. Jenny noted the label on the bag and the shoes. Married, Jenny deduced, and to someone who could afford to give her expensive clothes. And the woman had granddaughters, an experience Jenny would never have.

Except she might. Jenny looked forward to dinner with a one of the law partners in her firm who had lost his wife to breast cancer a year before. He had a daughter and several grandchildren. Jenny knew that if she let this older man pursue her, she would find herself organizing the grandchildren's visits to a spacious, well-appointed new home. She might even have to babysit. By herself.

"You know that's too wide for a scarf."

Jenny stopped and looked up to see the elderly woman staring at her knitting project. "I know."

"You makin' a shawl? A blanket for somebody?"

Jenny's carefully controlled mask of self-possession fell. "Yes, a prayer shawl."

The elderly woman nodded. "That's good, honey. Real good. Bless you, now."

Jenny watched the woman pass, slowly making her way to the escalator down to the commuter flights.

She knitted faster. She wanted to work on this piece more than anything. No, it wasn't a scarf at all. She had enough scarves. Everyone she knew had enough scarves.

She hadn't realized herself what she had started – another prayer shawl. The church she attended every couple of months collected pieces of knitting to give out to people they deemed "in need." Jenny decided this could be a way she could keep a foot in the door of a society she thought she might possibly need some day. Not now, of course. But the walls of the secure life she had built for herself could come tumbling down at any time. She might need to go to church someday.

Prayer shawls, Jenny had observed from the posters in the church hallway, were really big, wide scarves. Not much technique required. "The simpler, the better," one of the ladies managing the church prayer shawl ministry had told her.

Perfect, Jenny had thought. She knitted simple patterns primarily as stress relief anyway. She had chosen a couple of jumbo skeins of a fluffy pink, red, and purple variegated yarn and whipped out a comfy oversized scarf (or undersized blanket) that made the leader of the knitting guild smile in delight when Jenny presented it to her after church one Sunday.

She heard, a month or so later, that it had gone to a young woman, a professional dancer, in New York City. The girl had apparently attended the church as a child; her mother still faithfully showed up every Sunday. Jenny recognized the girl's mother as one of the church ladies who always greeted her with a big smile and a soft but heartfelt handshake at the Passing of the Peace, always acting glad to see her but never making any mention of Jenny's frequent absences from the church services. Jenny appreciated that.

Satisfied that her efforts had gone to a young woman with a career made Jenny feel good about donating her knitting to the church. She liked to think her first prayer shawl would encourage a young woman like herself, someone who had moved off to give herself the best opportunities available – something Jenny actually wished she had done herself.

So yes, I'm knitting another prayer shawl, Jenny said to herself. I'm making an effort to do my bit with a good group of women. I'm making a connection with nice ladies who have warm smile, don't judge me for my failures, and give heartfelt and soft handshakes.

"Flight 1961 to Knoxville, now boarding."

Jenny packed up her knitting, glided down the escalator to Gate 35A, and went home.

As she hoisted her suitcase off the carousel at the Knoxville airport, Jenny found herself face to face with the woman from church, the one with the ballerina daughter, the one with the friendly and welcoming smile.

"Well hello!" the woman exclaimed as soon as Jenny turned towards her. "What a coincidence. I'd like you to meet my daughter Samantha." She pointed towards a tall, thin young woman with impossibly long legs and long, dark hair.

Jenny gasped. "My prayer shawl!"

Samantha broke into a sweet, poignant smile as though she were meeting an old friend after a long absence. She reached to hug Jenny, the pink and purple prayer shawl draped over her long arms. "Thank you so much. You have no idea how much I needed this. It helped me get home."

Jenny stood looking up at the young woman, mystified, but feeling like something marvelous had just happened.

Done With It

Helen came out of the church ready for another fight – this time with God, or maybe with herself. Her friend Aggie followed her out the church office door, dragging with her at least as much frustration as her closest friend, the first friend she had made when she joined the church forty years before.

Helen got to her car, parked in the handicap space closest to the building, threw her folder of documents and writing pad filled with notes and curse words over onto the floor of the back seat, and lit a cigarette. Aggie plodded over, tired from all the arguing, and leaned against Helen's car. She sat her designer handbag gently on the hood of the car, reaching for a cigarette of her own.

"I'm done with it. Done with it all," Helen said.

"You've said that fifteen times before," Aggie drawled.

"This time I mean it," Helen snapped.

Aggie took a drag of her cigarette and did not respond.

This was not by any means the first after-meeting they had held in the church parking lot. In fact, the two women usually saved what they really wanted to say about All Saints Episcopal Church for the inevitable "parking lot meeting" after whatever official meeting they had just attended.

In the early days, they had bitched about the altar guild taking over precious table space back in the vestry, preventing them from doing their own work for the flower guild. When the far more solemn altar guild ladies got to the church first and shrugged off any requests for a little space for the flowers, Helen and Aggie always pasted rigid smiles on their faces, then vented in the parking lot after they finished their flower arrangements and got back to their cars, long after the altar guild had left.

As the church grew, they had held these after-meetings to de-brief Sunday School organizational meetings, planning meetings for the church bazaars, and the annual end-of-summer picnic and Rally Day. The times changed. Helen ran for a leadership position on the vestry of the church and won by a handful of votes. The women met regularly at the country club so that Aggie could share with Helen the latest outrages of her fellow vestry members. Aggie always picked at her salad and drank a cold glass of white wine, while Helen stress-ate a heavier meal, followed by dessert.

The weight alone, coupled with high blood pressure, had gotten Helen a blue handicap placard for what Aggie dryly referred to "movie star parking" right beside the doors of both the Club and the Church. Helen took this perk as her due, given the number of years she had performed hours of volunteer work of all kinds for the church (along with forty years of paying dues to the Club – and the Church, for that matter). But the close proximity of the car to the door sometimes made it hard to have her parking lot meetings with Aggie without the subjects of the meeting coming out right behind them, within earshot.

The two women stood by the car smoking for several minutes while the other members of the nursery school planning committee exited the buildings, waved their pseudo-friendly goodbyes, and walked on past. Aggie and Helen raised hands in waves but not much more.

"So what are we going to do?" Aggie asked. Her plan to use the church building for a nursery school for the children living in the low-income neighborhood immediately adjacent to the church had stalled out year after year. This time, with a formal committee appointed to look into the plan, she had hoped to finally get the nursery school off the ground. She knew how much money pre-school cost. She also knew young parents who worked at low-paying jobs didn't have it.

"Hell, I don't know," Helen said. "We're just trying to do something good for other people. I kinda sorta remember that being the purpose of church. Am I wrong?"

"You're right." Aggie looked in disappointment at her fellow committee members leaving in their Beemers and Mercedes. "Their grandchildren are enrolled in that Montessori school over on Kingston Pike as soon as they turn two." She remembered how she had enrolled her own children in a local kindergarten run by the Methodists as soon as they turned three. Motherhood had exhausted her. She needed a break. Her children likely needed a break from her, too. Part of growing up, she supposed.

She hadn't thought using the church building for a nursery school for low income children would be controversial. Honestly, she hadn't. But their longtime nemesis on the vestry of the church, Dottie Pearman, had vehemently opposed the plan, on the grounds that any use of the education wing of the church building would disrupt the church's Sunday School program. And then there was the matter of germs – and maybe the risk of lice, too.

"Oh, for God's sake," Helen had said as soon as these words came out of Dottie's mouth. "You think the poor kids are going to contaminate the few rich kids who still come to Sunday School?"

"This meeting is adjourned," Dottie had replied, shutting her file folder. "I'm not in favor of this, never have been. The church is for church members. We have to take care of our own."

Helen still fumed as Dottie finally came out of the church building and walked past them. Dottie pretended to get a phone call on her cell, conveniently ignoring Helen and Aggie. As soon as Dottie passed, Helen dropped her cigarette to the ground and snuffed it out with a stomp of her foot.

"I mean it, I'm done."

"I'm not there yet, but I understand." Aggie watched Helen search through her purse for her car keys.

She feared Helen really would finally leave the church this time. The two women had been through so much with this congregation – as young mothers, as energetic moms of school aged children with time on their hands and willing to take on church volunteer work, through the death of Aggie's daughter and then her husband, through Helen's increasing impatience with her homebound husband, coupled with impatience for just about anyone else who caused her frustration.

"Think it over," Aggie told her friend. "I'd miss you, you know."

Helen nodded. "We can still have lunch at the Club. Heck, maybe we wouldn't spend so much time bitching!"

When Helen pulled her car into the driveway, she remembered the file folder of plans for the nursery school and her note pad in the back seat. She didn't even want to look at the things. Pulling open the back door of the car, she gathered up the papers in a heap and dumped them straight into the garbage can beside the back door. She felt better.

She paced the kitchen, still angry, upset, frustrated over her church's failure to actually do what it said it should be doing. "Practice what y'all preach!" she called out to no one in particular.

Her legs hurt. She needed to sit down. She did not want to turn on the television and endure mindless prattling about celebrities she could care less about. Nor did she care to listen to the news shows, with other people yelling at each other or coming completely undone about political issues the everyday citizen realistically couldn't do anything about.

Helen stomped, awkwardly, into her little sewing room she had set up years ago to have some time to herself, away from the kids. She didn't particularly want to make anything. She had reached the age where she had a good, basic wardrobe that served her for any occasion. She neither needed nor wanted more clothes. And her boys were grown men and wouldn't wear anything their mother had made, even if she had a mind to make something for her own family.

Scuffling around in her closet of abandoned projects, she came across a pair of old metal knitting needles and a fat skein of bulky yarn. One winter years ago, she had taken up knitting and made everyone in the family hats and scarfs. She never did master mittens, and those tiny needles and thin yarn you had to use for socks completely exasperated her.

She had learned to knit only well enough to make hats. The hats she made for her boys looked chunky and basic. The shaping was usually skewed, and her seams often didn't quite line up. Once she completed them, her sons continually lost them. They probably ended up in the lost and found box at her sons' school. Helen had given up knitting hats long ago.

But scarves she could handle. Bind on, knit for as long as you've got yarn. Bind off. Tie up a loose end or two. If you got a yarn with a little color in it, you could get away with just knitting in basic garter stitch without bothering with a pattern. Helen picked up the old metal size nine needles and the fat skein of brown and green variegated yarn and hauled them off to her recliner in the family room.

Once she remembered the one tricky loop you had to make when you first started binding on, Helen's muscle memory kicked in and her hands took over from her mind, knitting along at a good pace. By the time she had knitted three rows, she paused, realizing she felt better, calmer. She had forgotten to think about the church meeting. She had forgotten to think angry thoughts or feel completely disillusioned with the whole mess.

Helen spent the rest of the afternoon knitting. Not thinking, not trying to figure anything out, not even remembering to go write out a letter of resignation from the church and every useless committee in it. She just knitted, one stitch at a time, row after row.

Each afternoon, after tidying up the house and starting the laundry, Helen found herself sitting down in her big recliner to knit. Sometimes she knitted for an hour or so at a time. Sometimes she just got in ten minutes before she needed to start dinner or take her husband to his physical therapy session. By the end of the week, she had a long, wide scarf complete and folded neatly on the family room table, ready to give to…somebody.

Helen stopped by the craft store and bought three more extra-large skeins of yarn, along with a nice set of wooden needles that looked cozier than her old metal ones from twenty years ago. That afternoon, she bound on for a new project, this time making the scarf extra wide – more of a shawl than a scarf.

She pondered what she could do with the scarves – or shawls, or whatever they were. She knew a group of biddies at church kept the clergy supplied with something they called "prayer shawls" to take to people in the hospital, or to hand out to people who had experienced a death in the family or what not. The gals in the prayer shawl guild never put their names on the things, just handed them over to the priests to make it look like the clergy had done some big thing. Typical, Helen thought.

Supposedly, the priests did some sort of "blessing" of the prayer shawls before handing them out. She'd heard one of the old biddies who knitted the things had a fit once, finding out that one of the lay pastoral care volunteers had taken a prayer shawl to somebody who had just checked into a nursing home without getting the thing officially "blessed" first. What hogwash, Helen thought.

She reckoned she could pray over a piece of knitting as well as anybody else. She ran through her growing circle of friends and acquaintances who had moved to assisted living, had a husband or wife confined to a nursing home, or just plain had bad health. And, she realized, none of these people went to church anymore. They wouldn't get a prayer shawl, like the official members of her church.

Did she dare? Helen decided she did. What could happen to her? She likely wouldn't be stricken by lightning, and if the priests found out and wanted to excommunicate her – fine. She considered carefully which of her friends might appreciate a short visit and a gift – and wouldn't think she was off her rocker for showing up unannounced with a piece of knitting. She decided on Harold St. Martin, an old guy who had lived down the street for the last thirty years. His wife had died two years ago, and Harold had just moved into an assisted living apartment across town. He had given up his driver's license when he moved to assisted living and likely couldn't attend church any longer. Helen felt embarrassed that she hadn't visited sooner.

Checking to make sure her husband had gone down for his afternoon nap, Helen rolled what she would now call her first "prayer shawl" out onto the family room table where she and her husband ate almost all their meals now. She placed both hands onto the long piece of knitting and took a deep breath.

She wouldn't pray out loud. She didn't feel confident enough in this endeavor to do that, at least this first time. So she prayed in her mind.

"Lord, bless this prayer shawl to give comfort to my neighbor Harold. Help him to know he is still remembered and loved. Help me to have a nice visit with him this afternoon and forgive me for not doing so earlier. In Christ's name, Amen."

There. Done. Helen felt better.

Three hours later, Helen got back into her car at the assisted living apartment complex to go back home. She felt tired, but tired in a good way, like she had been used for a good purpose. Harold had welcomed her in with honest delight that she had come to visit. He proudly draped the long knitted shawl over the back of the sofa where he sat most of the day to watch TV. Helen told him she missed him and wanted to visit. It wasn't until she was about to leave that she mentioned that the long scarf was a "prayer shawl" to let him know he was remembered by his old neighbors. Harold had dabbed at a tear welling up in his eye, thinking of his old neighborhood, and surely of his wife and their lives together, too.

Helen drove back home and collapsed into her recliner. She picked up her needles. She'd have maybe a half hour to work on her next prayer shawl.

Warmth

"Dad-gum, it's cold," Jimmy said to no one in particular. The cardboard fort he had built under the I-40 overpass in downtown Knoxville kept a little bit of the wind out, but that's about all.

Jimmy stretched in the frigid morning air and looked around. He needed something to eat. The mission kitchen that had fed him the night before wouldn't open for another couple of days. They'd given him a take-out bag with sandwiches and some energy bars, but he'd eaten those in the middle of the night, too cold to sleep.

A circle had formed around a fire in an old metal garbage can. Jimmy went over. He didn't quite know whether these city fellers would care to speak to him, but he'd try to find out where he could get a meal. He pulled his old brown jacket up around his ears and his black toboggan cap down around his neck. He knew he smelled bad, but he figured the other fellas over there did, too. He still hadn't found a place to get a bath.

Two of the fellas standing round the fire nodded to him. "Awful cold, ain't it?" he said to the group. All of them nodded, avoiding eye contact.

"Any y'all know where a feller could get a bite to eat this mornin'?"

None of the other men responded right off. Jimmy rubbed his hands over the fire and waited. He'd been in town long enough to know these folks in Knoxville didn't open up easy as they did back home.

"You fellers from around here?" he asked, looking around at the faces half-buried in their coats. He waited, feeling like a fool for talking out.

"Nah, nobody from here," a large man with dark skin and some kind of accent grumbled.

"I am!" a skinny man said. "Lived here all my life."

"Under the interstate, huh?" a young kid teased. Jimmy pegged the kid for a runaway. Likely everybody here had run away from somethin.'

"Naw, man, I lived up in Fountain City for thirty years. I ain't lived here but a month or so."

"Like six months, old man," the young kid said.

"Well, now, who's countin'?" the old guy replied.

"So where do ya get a bite to eat?" Jimmy repeated. If this old guy had lived here six months, he'd know where to go for a good meal.

"Aw, I go over there to the pantry on West Scott, when they open, which ain't ever' day," the old man told him.

"Yeah, they got bags to go, if you ask 'em," a man with dark frizzy hair told Jimmy. He stepped back from the fire. "I'm goin' over there, if you wanna go wit' me."

"Mighty kind of ya," Jimmy told him.

Jimmy followed the man, walking out from under the interstate and onto the cracked and uneven sidewalk, down past the mission building. "What's yor name? I'm Jimmy, from Fort Blackmore, Virginia."

Jimmy's new friend looked puzzled. Jimmy wondered if maybe people never introduced themselves down here in the city.

"Whatev,' man." The man hesitated, giving Jimmy the onceover before responding. "I'm Samuel," he said. "That's all you need to know, man."

"I reckon so," Jimmy said. He took the hint not to inquire further.

Samuel pointed to the opposite corner of the street, stepping out in front of a car, forcing it to stop to let the two men pass. "Down that street."

Jimmy sidestepped the car that had narrowly missed them, glad there weren't any more busy streets ahead. Samuel walked several paces ahead, towards a low grey building with a long, covered sidewalk along the side of it. Thirty or more folks stood in line, most of them scruffy looking men and a few women with little kids in tow. One old man with a white head of hair and beard sat on a white plastic chair at the head of the line. Jimmy couldn't figure out if he was somehow in charge or just got a chair on account of being old.

After several minutes of waiting in line with Samuel, the door to the building opened, and the people in the front of the line hurried inside. The old man at the head of the line got out of his chair and followed them.

"Give 'em a name," Samuel told him. "You don't need to tell 'em no more. They just give you stuff. You don't need to qualify for nuthin'."

Jimmy nodded like he understood, but he didn't. Somehow, he figured, he'd get something to eat inside. He and Samuel inched along. It seemed like the folks already inside sure took their time, whatever it was they were doing there.

As soon as they got to the door, a red-headed woman sitting at a small table handed a clipboard to Samuel. He signed it, then stepped away from Jimmy, joining another line at the back of the building.

"Good mornin'," Jimmy said to the woman offering him a clipboard.

"Good morning, sir," she replied. "Just jot your name down on the next line. Then you can go over and select what you'd like today. There's bread out back when you finish."

"Mighty kind of you," Jimmy said. The woman gave him another friendly smile and pointed to the line behind her.

Jimmy stepped over to the line, finding long tables piled high with frozen dinners, hundreds of cans of vegetables, plastic packages of meats, and dozens of choices of pastries like they sold in convenience stores. The men in front of Jimmy pointed to what they wanted, while clean-looking teenagers, all wearing red t-shirts saying "All Saints Youth Group," packed grocery bags for each person in line.

A grey-haired man with big round glasses, looking for all the world to Jimmy like an off-duty banker or lawyer or somebody of that ilk, stepped forward as Jimmy tried to figure out what he could reasonably ask for. The men in front of him had each pointed to two of the frozen dinners, and one of the teenage girls had told him sorry, he could only have one. But then she offered him three cans of some kind of spaghetti.

"Good morning," the man said to Jimmy. "We've got frozen dinners today, donated by one of the grocery stores in town. Maybe a chicken and dumpling dinner? Turkey and gravy?"

Jimmy looked down at his feet, intimidated by the man's crisp blue Oxford shirt and dress pants. His clean-shaven face and clean hair reminded Jimmy that he'd need to find someplace to wash off. "That's mighty nice of you, sir, but I ain't got no place to warm it up. It's awful cold out there."

The man gave Jimmy a slight nod. "One moment." He stepped aside to one of the teenage girls. "Do we still have a go-bag to give out?" he asked her quietly.

The pretty girl disappeared behind a row of boxes and came straight back with a big brown paper bag. "Here you are!" she said, handing the bag to Jimmy, as if he would know exactly what it was.

Jimmy slowly reached to take the bag. "Well now, I thank ye kindly, ma'am." She giggled for some reason and turned to help the next man in line.

Jimmy clutched the big paper bag to his chest, not knowing whether he was to continue in the line or whether he had gotten all he was to get. He opened the bag to take a peek inside, finding apples, crackers, and what looked like a ham sandwich down in the bottom. Another pretty teenage girl offered him a water bottle, and he took that. Nobody seemed to begrudge him taking that, in addition to what was in the bag.

The grey-haired man with the glasses now stood at the end of the line. "Help yourself to any of the desserts you'd like," he said to Jimmy. "And there's loaves of bread out back...might be good for sandwiches...I'll see if I can find you some peanut butter, too."

Jimmy followed the man out a side door to where more long tables piled high with bread loaves of all shapes and sizes stood ready for the taking. An elderly lady hobbled over to Jimmy and insisted he take a big loaf of bread with some kind of seeds on the top of it. She said it was a "gor-may loaf," like it was some kind of special something Jimmy should be glad to get ahold of.

"Here's a couple of jars of peanut butter," the grey-haired man called to him, coming out from what looked like a whole warehouse of food behind the smaller grey building. "You need something to carry all that?"

"That'd be mighty kind..." Jimmy began as the man walked off again.

He returned with a sturdy canvas bag and a big red blanket.

"Here you go." The man placed the extra-large sized plastic peanut butter jars in the bottom of the canvas tote, then added Jimmy's brown bag and the loaf of bread.

"And I thought you might be able to use this." He offered Jimmy the fluffy red blanket he had tucked under his arm.

Jimmy took the red blanket, unable to look the man in the face. Yes, he sure did need a good, warm blanket. He'd be able to wrap himself up good in that cardboard fort he'd made, and maybe he'd be a little warmer tonight. "Mighty kind of you, sir, might kind," he mumbled.

"My wife knitted it," the man said. "I know she'll be pleased that you'll put it to good use."

Jimmy wrapped the red blanket around his shoulders and took his time walking back to his fort under the interstate. He didn't try to make the cars stop on the busy street. He waited his turn, warm at last.

Inside his fort that night, Jimmy listened to the drunks howling and wrestling around the fire. He opened up a jar of peanut butter and spread it over a chunk of bread he'd pulled off the loaf. He chewed slowly, feeling something he hadn't felt since he'd left home – warmth.

Business Casual

Franny

"Hey Fran, got any more of those prayer shawls?"

Robert and I had gone through some re-adjustments since I had gone back to work…and his career had abruptly ended. When I heard him downstairs, asking me for prayer shawls, I was in the middle of putting on make-up, my mind already on the brief I needed to proof and file by noon.

"Ummm…there's one I just finished a couple of days ago downstairs. On the coffee table." I blotted my lipstick. Robert had appeared at the bathroom door, dressed in his new uniform of blue oxford cloth shirt and khakis. "I need to tie up loose ends, though."

"Tie up loose ends?" He sounded irritated.

I ran a brush through my hair. I needed to leave for work. Soon.

"You know…weave in the ends of the yarn where I cast on, cast off…I think I had a couple of places in the middle of the thing where I started a new skein."

Robert gave me an irritated pout. "Is that necessary?"

"Not unless you want strings hanging off of it. It won't look finished." I squeezed past him, looking for my purse.

"Could you do that now?"

I stopped and counted to five. "No, not really. I need to get to the office."

"Maybe I could do it..." he muttered.

"Hells bells." I found my purse, on the hearth of the fireplace in the TV room. My latest prayer shawl was on the coffee table, practically staring straight at me. It wouldn't take but a minute to tie up loose ends and call it finished.

I had given Robert a prayer shawl the day before, a fluffy red one, big enough to qualify as a blanket. I had in mind the church nursing home visitors could give it to someone to actually use as both a prayer shawl and an actual bed cover – something to brighten a room. But checking my personal emails (after two weeks of not having time to do so), I found I'd missed the collection deadline. I didn't want my work sitting around gathering dust in the church collection box, so I asked Robert if he could give it to someone at the food pantry.

"Sure," he said, holding it out for inspection. "But what is it?"

"It's a prayer shawl. You give it to someone to let them know you're thinking about them."

"It looks like a blanket."

"Well, it is a blanket."

"So why don't you call it a blanket?"

"Give it to someone you think needs thoughts and prayers. Surely to goodness you'll run across someone who meets those criteria at the food bank."

Robert started working at the food pantry a week after he lost his job. The first week, he had slept until mid-morning, depressed and without any clue of what to do with himself. He'd finally gone in to talk to one of the priests who'd suggested he spend some time volunteering at the food pantry the church ran near downtown. The pantry opened twice a week, letting anyone who needed food come and take enough to feed themselves and their families for three or four days. The pantry fed several hundred people a week and got local grocery stores to donate barely expired or about-to-expire food they couldn't sell.

Everybody in the congregation gladly donated money to the pantry. Maybe it was guilt. Maybe because nobody got a salary, and the money went straight to keeping the facility open and the food going out. A lot of the younger retired people in the congregation regularly worked there at least once a week.

After volunteering his first day, Robert had treated his work at the pantry like a job. He even got dressed as if he were going off to the office again, except he dressed in business casual rather than his usual suits and ties.

"I could probably do that," he said as I found my crochet hook and began weaving in the tail of yarn on the corner of the prayer shawl.

"It's fine. Least I could do."

"I gave away the red one yesterday," he said quietly as I scanned the blanket for loose ends in the middle, which were harder to see. "I thought about what you said, about finding somebody who needed thoughts and prayers."

"Oh? Do tell."

"This guy came in, you could tell he'd never been there before. He had this accent, like he'd come from up in the mountains somewhere."

"Maybe he did. Lot of poverty up there."

"Anyway, you could tell he didn't have a clue of what to do, what he could take, what the drill was. He came in with a guy named Samuel, who's there every time we're open. He never says anything. I've tried to make conversation with him, but he won't talk to any of us."

"I guess he has his reasons – or he's shy – or intimidated." I wove in the last loose end at the other corner of the prayer shawl. I held up the blanket, shook it out, and folded it neatly before handing it over to Robert.

"Hmm. Hadn't thought about that."

"We live in a different world than those people," I said.

"Guess you're right." He looked down at his own outfit, the oxford shirt with no tie as dressed-down as Robert ever got. He didn't even own a pair of sweat pants. He had one pair of jeans he wore once every six months.

"So you gave Samuel the red prayer shawl, or the guy with the mountain accent?"

"The mountain guy. He didn't take any of the food that had to be cooked, so I figured he was living on the street somewhere. We fixed him up with bread and peanut butter for sandwiches."

"That's nice."

"He seemed cold, too. So I got the prayer shawl for him. He was embarrassed, but he took it. I hope you don't mind?"

"It's fine," I said. My rush to get to work didn't seem so important now. But I did need to get to work. One of us needed a job. I grabbed my purse again and reached for the keys off the key rack.

"Hey Fran?"

"Hey what?" I tried to sound patient.

"Thanks for going back to work. I needed this – this time to do something that matters."

I smiled. "It's okay." I opened the door, determined not to get waylaid again. "Maybe I needed this, too."

"Have a good day." Robert tossed my new prayer shawl over his shoulder. "I'll find somebody who needs this."

Invitation to the Party

Clarissa

"Clarissa, there's some guy here to see you."

When one of the social workers leaned around the corner of my office to tell me this, I had no idea life was about to change.

I had gotten used to older, wealthy ladies dropping by from time to time, bringing prayer shawls to my clients. I had gotten used to women showing up at all hours, needing a place to stay and often with a couple of kids in tow. So the sight of a tall, polished man in his fifties, wearing a black suit and one of those Anglican dog collars, took me aback, to say the least.

"May I help you?"

"Will Henderson, I'm the rector of All Saints Church, over on the west side of town."

He flashed me a rather charming smile, and that gave me reason to put my guard up. "Are those prayer shawls for donation?" I pointed to the armful of knitted blankets he carried.

"Uh, yes," he said, almost as if he had forgotten why he had come.

"I'll take those." I reached for the prayer shawls, and he met me with another very charming smile.

"I hope the ladies here can use these," he said. "Our knitting guild works hard on them. What a terrific idea someone had to donate them to women here in the shelter."

"Sure was." I turned to place the shawls on a shelf until I could pass them around.

"And you are….?" He asked me.

This guy didn't seem to want to leave anytime soon. "Clarissa. Clarissa McCabe."

"So nice to meet you." He reached his hand out, and I took it reluctantly. I really, really, did not want to get into a discussion with a preacher. I believed what I believed, and I didn't care to discuss those beliefs with anyone else. But he might be useful in getting more donations to the center. "I'm the director here."

"So I assumed. Have we met before?"

"No, no. I don't think so." I hoped he hadn't seen me coming or going from my meetings at his church.

The Reverend Henderson frowned. "Maybe coming or going, just in passing?"

"No, I don't think so."

He paused for a several moments. "Listen, I'm trying to track down someone. Someone who knits these prayer shawls for my church."

I made no response.

He hesitated, waiting for me to fess up. "The thing is, someone made the most exquisite knitted prayer shawls we've ever had donated to us. They're gorgeous! And we don't know who this person is. I've asked around, and none of the regular knitting guild members know anything about them. They admire them, of course, but no one can say who made them."

He waited for me to say something. I searched his face, trying to figure out what he might know about me…and how (and if) he had figured out that I had donated the prettiest, most intricately designed prayer shawls in the donation box.

Will Henderson fidgeted. "And I really need to find out, because there's this woman in our church, Mrs. Tyson, who is our largest donor – by far – and she received one of these prayer shawls, and she really, really wants to meet the person who made it."

"I see."

"She's having a party soon – for new members of the church – and she'd like the person who made the prayer shawl to come as a special guest."

"But you don't know who this person is."

"No, I don't. At least, not for sure."

I felt a little sorry for this guy. He knew I'd made that prayer shawl. A major donor was putting the squeeze on him to meet the creator of it. I'd been in fundraising enough to know he had found himself in a pinch.

"What makes you think you might find the person who knitted Mrs. Henderson's prayer shawl here?"

"This is awkward." He rubbed his hands together nervously. "I asked around the office, and no one, not the church secretary, the volunteers, the maintenance guys – no one had a clue of who had put such beautiful work in the donation box. I even made an announcement at the worship service, hoping someone would come forward. So…."

"How do you find me?"

He winced. "I checked the security cameras. One of the volunteers recognized you from when she brought the last batch of prayer shawls over."

"You didn't! Those meetings are supposed to be confidential!"

"I'm so sorry."

I paced my office, outraged that a member of the clergy would breach my anonymity as a member of a recovery group. "I wish I had never donated a stitch of my knitting to your church." I said that to hurt him. Taking up knitting again had made me so much calmer, so much more able to stay off pills, alcohol, all of it.

"Could we start this conversation over again?" the priest asked.

"You wish," I hissed.

"I've screwed this up so bad."

I shot him an angry look. "Okay. So you know. And you know I dropped those shawls off on the way to my recovery group."

"Hey, it's nothing to be ashamed of. In fact, I admire you, going to meetings, taking charge of your life."

I scowled at him, though I began to want to lighten up on him. "Many of us who go to those meetings think your good church people will get all judgmental on us."

"I'm not one of them. Quite the contrary."

My eyes met his in a moment of true honesty. "Okay. I accept that."

"We all have our demons," he said quietly.

"True enough. So. Let's start this conversation over again."

He invited me to an event he called a "Newcomer's Social" the following Friday evening at Mrs. Tyson's house in the posh part of town. He confessed to telling the elderly woman that I was one such newcomer to the church, and he said Mrs. Tyson had decided I was just the kind of new church member she hoped would join her beloved church. She couldn't wait to meet me.

"I can pick you up?" the Reverend Henderson suggested.

"That's not necessary." This guy made me nervous.

"Honestly, it's the least I can do."

So I agreed, mostly because I didn't want to show up at a party in the nicest part of town in my old beater of a car. And yes, this was the least this guy could do, given what I reminded myself was indeed a rather outrageous breach of my confidentiality.

Will Henderson picked me up in a Mercedes with more than a few miles on it, parking it outside my apartment building and hustling up the steps to my door five minutes before our designated pick-up time. He flashed his charming smile and took my hand in a gentle shake.

I had dressed up as much as I ever dress up – which is to say I wore an ankle length, floaty peasant skirt and a cotton top, both pilfered from the donation box at the center. I wore scuffed sandals and some beaded bracelets to jazz myself up a bit. I thought about putting my hair in an up-do, but in the end, I left it wild, curls hanging loose. I am who I am, I reminded myself.

We didn't speak much in the car. What do you say to a priest when he's picking you up for a party? He seemed a little edgy, too, so I didn't try too hard to make conversation.

We arrived at a brick mansion at the end of a narrow, winding driveway lined with willow trees fluttering in the breeze. After leaving the car with a valet hired for the event, I followed Will to the door of a large brick house with an oversized oak door. He gave the door a brief knock and walked on in.

At the end of the long entryway, beside a wall of mullioned glass panels, a shriveled old woman with white hair pinned back with a diamond-encrusted barrette sat in a wheelchair, ready to welcome her guests. Will stopped to gently push me in front of himself, presenting his prize to his benefactor.

"Why Fatha Henderson…who's this pretty lady you've brought he-ah tonight?"

"May I present Clarissa McCabe, Mrs. Tyson. She's the one who knitted your beautiful prayer shawl."

The old lady's bony hands reached out to take mine. She held them for several moments, looking up at me with such gratitude in her rheumy old eyes. I didn't know what to say, what to do. I looked to Will for help.

"Mrs. Tyson was so touched to receive your prayer shawl, Clarissa."

The old lady kept holding onto my hands, nodding, weeping. "I can't tell you how much…" she began, but couldn't finish.

"It was my pleasure, Mrs. Tyson. It helped me, too."

She finally let go of one of my hands to pull an embroidered handkerchief off her lap and dab at her eyes. "You are very gifted, my dear. Very gifted. Thank you so much."

I squeezed her hands. She finally let go of me, and Will patted her shoulders in a sort of benediction. "We'll let you greet your other guests, Mrs. Tyson."

"Thank you for coming, my dears. I do appreciate you coming so much," she said, smiling at me.

Will ushered me into a spacious room with full length windows overlooking the Tennessee River. Tables had been placed along the windows, laden with hors d'oeuvres of puff pastries, deli meats, and fresh fruit. At the end of each side of the room, uniformed wait staff stood ready to serve champagne and punch.

"This is some church picnic," I commented.

"It's over the top, I agree. But Mrs. Tyson wants to put on the dog when it comes to welcoming new people to her church. She doesn't believe in going halfway."

"I'll say."

We mingled for the next hour or so. I had to admit, the people I met welcomed me with warm smiles and listened with genuine interest when Will told them I directed a shelter for abused women downtown. Some of them even asked for my business card, promising to send a donation.

"I'm glad I came to this," I told the reverend as we walked down the willow tree-lined driveway to his car.

"So am I."

We strolled down the driveway at a companionably pace, listening to the cicadas in the cool evening air. I suddenly got this crazy idea that I actually enjoyed spending time in this man's presence. It wasn't anything he said, just that I felt safe, felt something almost like peace and contentment.

"You have anything planned for the rest of the evening?" he asked me. "Wanna go for a coffee or something?"

No, no, no, I told myself. "I should let you get back to…whatever you do on Friday nights."

Will, strolling along, hands in his pockets, began whistling a song, something that sounded like an old hymn. He finished the song before responding. He stopped and looked at me. "I don't have anything planned."

"No…family? Wife?"

"Divorced," he said.

"Oh." We walked to the car. He drove me home in a tense silence.

"Can I see you again?"

"Of course," I said quietly. Before things got any more uncomfortable, I waved goodbye and rushed upstairs to my apartment. Nearly breathless and feeling nervous about the whole situation, I paced the living room before making myself sit down and pick up the knitting needles.

Casting on with a new red silk yarn I had just bought the week before, I started a new prayer shawl. This one was for me. And maybe Will Henderson, too.

Abby Learns to Knit

Abby

My bishop decided I needed a lesson in humility. And in the deepest part of my soul, I had to admit he had a point.

I arrived at the weekly Friday morning meeting of the Knitting Guild armed with two knitting needles, a skein of blue yarn, and more intimidated than I'd felt since my first year of seminary. I'd make a fool of myself. I knew that. And I'd have to learn from these women who - again, in the deepest reaches of my soul - I privately regarded with a little bit of condescension and a lot of ingratitude.

"So good to see you, Abby," Melba Strickland drawled as I walked in.

Martha Craig, the deacon, simply nodded at me. I'd asked the congregation to call me Mother Abby, and the deacon had met that request with utter silence and a blank face. I hadn't pressed the issue.

"I hope you ladies brought your patience," I chirped.

"You can do this. We have faith," Martha told me. I wondered if she had said something to the bishop. She acted a bit too eager to help with my lesson in humility.

"Let's tackle casting on first." Melba pulled up a chair beside me. "This first knot you have to make is the trickiest thing you'll do all day." She wrapped a piece of yarn around her thumb and did this maneuver that took me fifteen tries before I got it.

A half hour later, I had finally cast on one line of little loops onto one needle. I wanted to quit. I prayed that a parishioner would have some emergency requiring me to leave the yarn, the needles, the two older women – all of it – never to return.

"Maybe that's enough for today?" I suggested.

"You're just getting started," Melba told me. I glanced towards my phone, but it remained dark and silent. I wasn't getting out of this.

"Go back through the stitch, wrap the yarn around, then push down on the right needle and off the left needle."

It took me a full ten seconds to make one stitch. At this rate, I might finish my first prayer shawl before I retired. But finally, I picked up speed. Melba quietly left me alone to practice. Before I knew it, I'd knitted my first row.

"Now, just do it all again. That's called the garter stitch."

I nodded, flipped my fledgling project around, and knitted another row.

"You're picking this up quickly. Let's teach you to purl now." Melba had me jab my needle through the front of the stitches this time, making a bumpy row of stitches on the front of project. After Melba had guided me through a row of knit stitches, followed by a row of purls, I found my work looking like...well, real knitting.

Martha looked at me with something that I took as respect as I packed up my two-inch long piece of knitting to go home and work on it by myself. This hadn't been so bad after all. Once I had gotten the hang of the stitches, I actually felt myself settling into the mindlessness of it and enjoyed not having to do anything more taxing with my mind. I thanked God for not answering my prayers, glad that the phone hadn't rung before I had begun to make the stitches without having to stop to think about them.

I had the rest of the day off. Or at least I didn't have to be in the office. None of the church staff worked on Friday afternoons. Everyone rushed around in the morning to get ready for the Sunday services (and meetings and classes and whatever else came at us during a jam-packed schedule). So we all took Friday afternoons off to make up for working hard on Sundays. The clergy were presumably working on sermons.

That presumably included me. The rector had put me on the schedule to preach for the early service, and I hadn't done more than glance at the scripture readings for the day. I should have gotten down to some serious thinking about my sermon as soon as I got home, but I found myself taking my knitting project out to the sun porch off the back of my little house instead.

The church let me live for free in the old rectory purchased for the priest and his family fifty-odd years ago. In the 1980's, the church had bought a larger house in a better neighborhood for the rector, relegating this two-bedroom cottage a block away from the church building for use by an assistant priest. It was so small (and in an increasingly sketchy neighborhood), that only priests right out of seminary agreed to live there.

But it suited me fine. After living in not much more than mud huts while I served in Africa, a compact cottage with running water, a twin bed, and extra room for an exercise bike in the guest room seemed like a luxury. The kitchen was the biggest room in the house, but it didn't have a dishwasher. The appliances were thirty years old. But I didn't have to share the house with anyone else, and few of the church members sought me out, intimidated by the drug dealers living across the street and the non-English speaking neighbors living on both sides of me.

Usually, I wrote my sermons on the old yellow brocade sofa in the living room, with a Bible propped up beside me and my laptop perched on a sofa cushion. But the room felt stuffy, and honestly, I just didn't feel like working on my sermon yet.

The sun porch had flaky paint and a rusted porch swing hanging by chains from the wooden ceiling, but with screens on three sides of it, I got a nice breeze and a view of nothing but trees. I poured myself a glass of iced tea and climbed onto the porch swing with my new knitting project.

I knitted. That's all I did.

I realized I had zoned out, completely forgetting about my sermon, about the bishop's ragging on me to learn humility, about all the parish politics that usually drove me crazy.

My mind wandered back to the hot and humid little village I lived in during my time in Zambia. The relief organization I'd worked for sent me out on something akin to a listening tour to "assess the entrepreneurial needs of local women" struggling to put food on the table for their families. The local families (often run by single women) had welcomed me, offering me a mat to sleep on and vegetables and maybe a little chicken to eat.

One of the women considered a "success" by the development agency, Salma, worked as a sculptor, quarrying her own stone and making small works she sold through the agency's online store. I bunked with her for several days, tagging along with her to find stone, hack it out of the ground, and cart it back to her hut.

Salma worked hard – too hard, I thought. I couldn't figure out the appeal of spending an entire day quarrying the stone for her projects. At one point, I even suggested she sub out this work to men or young boys in the village. I saw it as a development and expansion opportunity for both Salma and the men in the village. But she gave me a nasty look and ignored me.

I trudged out with her the next day, bored out of my skull and impatient as hell, to watch her painstakingly dig stone out for her sculptures. I couldn't understand why she didn't spend more of her time on the creative part of her work – making an actual piece of artwork.

But as I realized I'd spent an hour of my own time doing nothing more than slip loops of yarn over each other, I began to understand Salma and her stone quarrying. She had never said a word to me or anyone else while she quarried the stone. In fact, I got the impression she really wished I hadn't come along. She let slip a tiny look of satisfaction when I told her I'd need to move along to the next village on my stop.

Thinking back on Salma working in the dust, slowly chiseling out her stone, I realized she had the same zoned-out, but peaceful, look on her face as she worked that I likely had on my face as I knitted.

"Peace, be still!" The words of the scripture I was supposed to preach on suddenly popped into my mind. And there was my sermon, as plain as day in my mind. I would tell the story of Salma and her stone quarrying, working in silence and in peace. I would contrast her quiet, seemingly boring work that resulted in profoundly spiritual artwork to the stressed-out, chaotic, profit-driven culture of America.

I knitted a few more rows. My work for Sunday morning was done, even though I hadn't intended to work this afternoon at all.

The next Friday, I showed up for the Knitting Guild meeting with a long piece of knitting in a warm, cozy shade of blue. Martha showed me how to cast off (which I found much easier than casting on) and tie up the loose ends of yarn at the bottom and top of my work. Melba led a round of applause for me (which I'm sure my bishop would not have appreciated) and made a big production of folding up my work and adding it to the stack of prayer shawls ready for distribution.

"Why don't you go ahead and bless them?" Melba told me.

For once, I didn't mind being bossed around by one of the older ladies. I felt I had earned the privilege of doing something liturgical for the rest of the group.

I placed my hands over the stack of prayer shawls for the blessings, and before I began, I asked the rest of the group to join me. We all stood, pressed together in a tight group, all with our hands lightly touching the prayer shawls.

Noticing Martha's large frame hanging back, letting the other ladies step in front of her to lay their hands on the prayer shawls, I thought how she had knit so many of these prayer shawls, visited so many patients in the hospital, and tended to the everyday spiritual needs of all the women in the parish, long before I had even entered seminary.

"Martha, would you mind leading us in this blessing?" I asked.

Martha looked up from a moment of private contemplation in surprise. "Certainly," she said. She stepped forward and added her large hands to the rest of ours.

"The Lord be with you."

"And also with you!" we responded.

Martha took a deep breath and led us in a long moment of joyful silence before beginning her blessing of the prayer shawls.

"Lord, we thank you for the joy of knitting. We thank you for peaceful moments of simple work. We thank you for peaceful moments of fellowship with You and with each other. Bless these prayer shawls to the healing and peace of those who receive them. Help them to know the joy of quiet time with you and with others. In Christ's name, Amen."

Behind my closed eyes, I felt tears welling up. As I opened my eyes to the sight of all the women reaching to hug me, to hug each other, I let the tears fall. And no one needed to ask me why. I finally felt like I belonged in this congregation.

Before I left, Melba gave me a bag of ultra-soft grey cashmere yarn someone in the parish had donated to the Knitting Guild. As soon as I got home, I settled myself into the porch swing and cast on. I didn't know what I'd make. I decided to knit like a sculptor – finding out what the project would become as I went along.

Fair Linen at the Beach

Will thanked God he had a room to himself at Melba Strickland's beach house. She insisted the vestry hold its annual retreat at her vacation home on Folly Beach, South Carolina. Will doubted anything of substance would get done.

"Father Will, dinner's at six!"

Will sighed and continued unpacking his dress-casual shorts and polo shorts. "Can't wait!" he called back cheerfully.

He hoped the rest of the group would assume he had reverent things to attend to, alone in his room. Really, he just needed some space. The vestry comprised eleven "active seniors" (as he had learned to call elderly people who winced at the term "elderly") and one young woman, Judith, who insisted she felt the call to the priesthood. Will actively supported her campaign for election to the vestry. Within six weeks in office, he reckoned, she'd get the gist of what real church work entailed.

Ostensibly to save expenses, one of the old codgers on the vestry, Ed Anderson, had rented a huge passenger van to drive them all to the beach. Though Will had nabbed the back corner for himself, the trip became (as he expected) a bad synthesis of a day at a senior center and a hippy road trip from the seventies. All the talk of everyone's arthritis and other assorted ailments, all the talk of what a lousy job the government did to help the poor, all the talk of booze and food they would consume at the beach house –

Will wanted to leap out of the van by the time Ed began his nausea-inducing lane weaving through the curvy, steep sections of I-40 through the Smoky Mountains, just outside Knoxville.

Will glanced at his watch, noting he had a good forty-five minutes before dinner. How rude would it be to slip out for a walk on the beach? Not rude, but a necessity, he decided.

"I'll going out for some meditative time," he firmly explained to the group gathered around whisky sours and crackers in the beach house living room. They all nodded respectfully, and no one tried to stop him or ask to join him - one of the times Will found it useful that few people understood exactly what a priest did. He heard Judith holding forth on ecclesiology as he padded out the back door in his bare feet. By the time he reached the end of the walkway to the beach, he could breathe freely and dropped all pretense of putting up with the vestry for a weekend.

He walked with the sun at his back on the edge of the surf. On a late Sunday afternoon, the weekend tourists had mostly cleared out. Two small children splashed in a tide pool while their mom held an e-reader close to her face. Way down the beach, towards Kiawah, a guy dressed in white from head to toe cast off with a tall fishing pole and retreated to an old-fashioned lawn chair. Will figured he could walk about that far and get back before dinner.

He really needed to pray about this retreat, he told himself. Between the finances and the sudden drop in parishioners' willingness to volunteer for the myriad of church duties that kept the place running, the state of the church did not look good. He'd have to tell them that. He'd have to somehow make the vestry face reality. He hoped they wouldn't simply take it out on him. Vestries did that sometimes. If pledges dropped, they'd blame the rector. If people stopped coming, they'd blame the rector for that, too.

But Will knew he couldn't be blamed for what the church was going through. When he had graduated from Virginia Seminary back thirty years ago, maybe you could blame the clergy for not filling "butts in the pews and dollars in the plate." People still went to church back then. You advertised your programs and big events in the paper. You asked people to invite their friends. You welcomed the visitors. If you could come up with a decent sermon and make sure the newcomers got a fair amount of attention, your church would grow.

That time had passed. Now, the only visitors who ever showed up were older people who had moved to town to retire. They lived on social security and pensions, most of them, and couldn't reasonably part with big chunks of change for the donations the church depended upon. The few middle-aged couples who still attended had their children's college bills to pay and laughed when asked if they could spare anything for the church. One smart-mouthed guy even asked Will if the church could spare some scholarship money for his kid going to medical school. "Cure the sick, right? Well, help us out!" the guy had said.

Will couldn't argue with him. If he and Sandy had been able to have children, he'd be in the same boat. Halfway down the beach towards the old guy with the fishing rod, Will stopped and faced the ocean. He took deep breaths in and out, trying to let go of all his anxieties about the vestry retreat and the difficult conversations he knew they needed to have. He looked out onto the vast Atlantic Ocean and reminded himself that he was but a small part of God's creation. In the end, the immensity of God, the immensity of time and even of the planet Earth, dwarfed whatever small problems his little church faced. He exhaled once more, imagining all his worries released to the universe, unto God.

He resumed his walk, feeling better, finding himself thinking about Clarissa McCabe and the work she did at the women's shelter. She ran that place mostly by herself, he thought. Surely she got grants and donations and large gifts to fund her work. Surely she had some sort of board of directors to report to. But from what he understood, she pretty much spent the bulk of her time tending to the souls who needed her. She truly did full time ministry, as opposed to squeezing it in between endless unproductive meetings and socializing, as he did.

Will kicked a shell down the beach in frustration. He'd known what he was getting into by the end of his first year of seminary. He'd accepted the fact that he'd have to deal with church politics, show up places and smile for photos at silly fundraising events, that he'd have to mix and mingle with other clergy every so often and have to suffer the inevitable, jealousy-laden comparisons between gigs that always went on at clericus meetings and conferences.

But he always thought the crux of his work would be true ministry to those in need. He felt that in his heart. He had, so far, pushed all that crap out of his way to always, always find time for hard core ministry.

Until lately. Will winced as he stepped on a jagged shell. A divine sign that he had become nothing but a grumpy, disillusioned old priest and needed a sharp and unexpected whack of pain in order to feel anything like a true emotion, he decided. He deserved it.

Maybe I need a change, he found himself thinking. He could work for a non-profit that actually accomplished something on behalf of poor people. He had the necessary skills for that. He didn't need a clerical collar to do something like that. He didn't need to quote the Bible or carry around a prayer book to do ministry, true ministry, he told himself.

Will carried this thought with him as he approached the man with the fishing rod. The man's wrinkled face crinkled up in a warm smile as Will approached. A big white plastic bucket of fish and water stood in the sand beside him. Will caught a whiff of it as he waved to the old guy.

"How's the fishin' today?" he asked the man.

"Not bad for the end of a day," the fisherman replied in a South Carolina drawl. "Not bad at all. And yourself?"

"Just takin' a breather," Will told him. "I'm not much of a fisherman."

"Well, now, you don't know that," he old guy said.

Will chortled. "I guess I'd do as well with fish as I do with people," he said.

The fisherman reeled in a fish as Will stopped to watch him. "It's all the same. Fish, people. All the same. You put out bait for 'em. Something you think they'll like. Some take it. Some don't. You take the ones that come to you and help ease them on their way. Some you throw back, not their time yet. S'all it is."

Will continued watching as the old man inspected the fish in his hands and pitched it back in the water. "Why'd you throw it back?" he asked.

"Got all I can handle," he said. "You don't need all the fish in the world to make a good dinner. Just what you can handle, just what you can handle for your own self."

Will nodded, waved goodbye, and continued his walk. He felt better. His mind had cleared. He couldn't handle all the fish in the world, but maybe he could handle the few "fish" waiting for him back at the beach house.

He got to the end of the beach, right across from Kiawah Island, and he turned back. The old fisherman, carrying his catch and fishing rod back towards the dunes, waved to him and disappeared into the grasses as they fluttered in the wind.

"Let's try to think of a metaphor for our parish," Will suggested. The vestry members had taken seats in the large screened-in porch overlooking the ocean. Melba had switched her beverage selection to peach flavored iced tea, served with the local cheese straws everyone loved. Will passed on both, eager to get on with the business of the vestry retreat.

No one spoke for several moments. Ed Anderson got up to pass around a fresh box of cheese straws. Melba excused herself to get a pitcher to refill the iced tea glasses. Will hoped he hadn't lost their attention.

"What about a hospital?" Melba suggested as she filled Judith's iced tea glass. "Could that be a metaphor we could work with?"

"Yes," Will said, taking the bait. "That's a perfect metaphor. Now, what does that mean for us as leaders of the church?"

"We create hassles for people?" Judith joked.

Uncomfortable laughter erupted. Will frowned.

"Ok. We may have to own that one," he said. "But what else?"

"We're in the healing business."

"And some people need us more than others."

"Father Will, could we talk about that expanded newcomers' ministry Mrs. Tyson offered to fund?" Melba Strickland asked.

Will tried not to show how irritated this interruption made him feel. "Yes, Melba. We'll get to that. But could we stay with this metaphor for a moment?"

Melba took a sip of her iced tea and set it down on a driftwood side table with a thump. "I think we need to talk about keeping our church afloat."

Will glanced around at each of the vestry members. They all stared back at him. Clearly, they all agreed with Melba's insistence that they speak of actual issues, not what Melba had once termed "hippy dippy, touchy-feely stuff."

"Ok," he said.

The tone of the room relaxed at once. "I understand you wantin' to go through all that theological stuff, reverend," Ed Anderson said. "But we've all been around the block a time or two. We kinda know where each other's comin' from. I think we just want to take care of some business and get on with it," he said, not unkindly.

Will nodded his head. "Sure. That's fine," he said. "I should have realized that." He had learned long ago as a rector to freely apologize for things he didn't exactly feel sorry about at all. "I just wanted to present a formational piece to the discussion," he added.

Most of the vestry members nodded in sympathy. "Maybe those of us who want to explore deeper into the theology of what we do can meet later," Judith suggested.

"All right," Will said, "so let's talk about this newcomer's initiative. When's the next party?"

"Mrs. Tyson is thinking a late spring, early summer thing." Melba took the ball and ran with it.

"We're thinking about the time school is over and people have more time."

"Yeah, but everybody's on vacation then…."

"How are you going to get names and addresses?"

Will allowed himself a tiny sigh. The vestry had hijacked his attempts to focus on the big picture of their work as a church, once again. They would now argue back and forth about the details and minutiae of their next social gathering. They would continue as they always had, working under the assumption that all they had to do was offer drinks and cake to the next crop of new members eager to sign up for weekly church services, full volunteer commitments, and their names on the dotted lines of the yearly pledge cards.

But that ship had sailed. No one went to church any more. Not the young and middle-aged parents of tots and teens that had once filled the pews of every church in America, anyway. Will scanned the grey and white heads of the vestry members seated around him. They had always known the "Church Triumphant," the church of the nineteen fifties, where everyone in town belonged to a congregation and could be well pigeon-holed as belonging to one of the mainstream Protestant denominations.

That had all changed. He had tried, gently, to help them face this fact. But as they tossed around ideas of the next newcomer's social at the church benefactor's home, he suddenly realized that they simply didn't want to face the new reality. They didn't want to think past the church they had always known. In their hearts and minds, the neighborhood parish church would always be the place they spiritually and emotionally called home. Until they died. Until it was too late.

Will reached for his iced tea and took a long, slow sip. He pretended Melba had spiked it with a good dose of vodka and let his mind and body relax into a state of acceptance and surrender. This is where this group was. There was nothing he could do to change the situation. There was nothing to do but serve as their pastor and their friend.

"So we have a plan," Melba announced. "Is that all okay with you, Father Will?"

He smiled a genuine smile. "That's all sounds fine. Good work."

The vestry retreat had concluded. For their final session together, Will set up a table as an altar on the back deck of the beach house for the celebration of Holy Communion. He left room for the vestry members to stand before the altar, a view of the Atlantic Ocean in the background.

The table looked bare, too much like the picnic table it was. "I've got just the thing," Melba told him when he asked if she had a nice white tablecloth he could use.

She came back with a white, lacey, knitted cloth that covered most of the weathered picnic table. After she spread it out, Will thought about the first time he had seen Clarissa in the parish office, about the pretty yellow prayer shawl she had knitted. Maybe she had knitted this one as well?

Melba hurried back to the kitchen and returned with a loaf of whole wheat bread for their celebration, covered in a red and white gingham cloth, still warm from the oven. Will transferred it to a handmade ceramic plate Melba had provided as a paten, while she filled a matching handmade chalice with a special red wine she had brought to the beach with her.

After the vestry members gathered in front of the altar, Will raised his arms to the sky to welcome them. "The Lord be with you!"

"And also with you," they responded. Behind Will, the old fisherman walked along the beach, looking for just the right place to set up his fishing rods.

Will held up the fresh bread to break it, and he felt the presence of the Holy Spirit among them. As Melba helped stepped forward to help with the chalice of deep burgundy-colored wine, Will glanced down at the knitted prayer shawl covering the makeshift altar. He wanted to do something tangible that meant something to people, just like the prayer shawl that meant so much to Mrs. Tyson. That's what he needed to do. A new call? Yes, he felt himself drawn to a new call, of some kind.

As he served each vestry member with a good-sized chunk of bread, Will felt himself filled, almost afloat, with gratitude for this time at the beach. He felt a clarity he hadn't felt in a long time, a release of worry and anxiety.

The vestry members filed off to finish packing and head back home. Will took one more short walk along the surf. He wondered how Clarissa and her work fit into this new sense of peace he felt. Maybe he was called to do something similar.

As he took one last look at the ocean, he waved to the fisherman far down the beach, even though the guy couldn't possible see him. He promised himself to actively discern where – or to what - he might next be called. He pledged to find the same sense of calm satisfaction and purpose as that old guy down the beach.

The Quiet One

Nan

At the breaking of the Host, I felt a shiver run through my body. When it was my turn to follow the parishioners to the altar rail to receive Holy Communion, I held back, letting everyone else go ahead of me.

As I held up my upturned hands to receive the small chunk of bread, I turned my eyes up to the young female priest. "Nan, this is the Body of Christ, given to you." That surprised me. I didn't think any of the clergy knew my name.

Not that I tried to attract attention to myself. To most people, I was simply one of the fixtures on the back pew, a thin woman with long grey hair pulled back into a limp ponytail, a plain face.

And that suited me. I didn't want any attention. I just wanted to sit in the back and be with God.

The moment I stepped into this Church, I felt I was home. I had strayed from Christian community since my twenties, and I knew I needed to return. I didn't want the church of my parents. I didn't want a church that judged me and told me I would go straight to hell, no matter what I did. I wanted love from a community that embraced me. I wanted to belong.

I signed up for the Inquirer's Course the very next Sunday. I loved that class – all the history, all the energy of others new to the faith, the patient answers and responses to hard questions from the clergy. I didn't want it to end.

A new year-long Bible study started a few weeks later, and I signed up immediately. I could finally wrestle with questions I'd had all my life. Why do people suffer? Why do the rich seem to get all the benefits of life while the poor get very little? What is my purpose in life? What gives anyone's life meaning?

The other women in my class became my close friends. We talked about topics that mattered. We were honest with each other, really honest. We heard about boyfriends and husbands, miscarriages, divorces, loss of jobs, and loss of children. We heard the pain of having been scorned by other churches, along with stories of amazing redemption. We cried at times. We laughed. We celebrated new babies and new jobs and gave God thanks for all of them.

At the end of the class, we were asked to sign up for a ministry. We were asked to "discern" God's call to us. All of the other women had a passion for something. One woman loved working with children and signed up as a Sunday School teacher. Another woman felt called to work with the food pantry offering canned vegetables, unsold frozen meals, and day-old bread to anyone who walked in off the street, hungry and no place else to go. Yet another woman felt called to visit nursing homes, spending time with the lonely residents there.

But me? I didn't feel "called" to anything. I didn't have a "passion" for any of the official ministries in the church. I knew everyone needed to do something to support the work of the church. Abby, the young female priest, spoke about her work in sub-Saharan Africa and the women there starting their own little gardens to grow food for their families and maybe some extra vegetables to sell for cash, too. Mother Abby spoke of how once she had become aware of the needs in Africa, she knew she was called to do something about the situation. She went on this big, huge adventure and did so much good.

That wasn't me. I took a Gifts & Talents inventory, a kind of test that was supposed to tell you what you might be called to do. It was supposed to help you identify skills you could use to minister to others. The only skill I listed was that I could knit.

My grandmother taught me to knit thirty years ago. When the prayer shawl ministry began, a hint of a delicate call to this ministry arose in my heart. I could do that. I could get some inexpensive yarn, and I could knit for people.

Knitting became part of my spiritual journey. I thought of it as a kind of active meditation, a time when I could check out of the world around me for a few minutes and become part of the spiritual universe. Sometimes I actively prayed while I knitted. Knowing my work would go to someone in need, I prayed for the recipient of the work. I prayed for myself and for what I could perhaps do for that person, spiritually or in a more tangible form.

"Take Bessie one of those new prayer shawls, why don't you?" the church secretary called to Will Henderson as he headed towards the door for his hospital rounds.

"Good idea," he replied, re-tracing his steps back to the cabinet where the church stored prayer shawls for distribution.

He chose a deep red blanket, one of the larger prayer shawls, obviously one knitted with a lot of generosity for the ministry. "I think I'll take her this one. It should go to a special person."

The church secretary nodded in agreement. "Bessie's so sweet. Always there when we need her. Always bringing a pie or a casserole whenever we have a dinner. And you know she's an original member of the altar guild?"

"I'm not surprised," the priest replied. He fingered the stitches of the red prayer shawl. So simple, yet so intricate, too, he thought. He folded the prayer shawl into a neat square and clipped a tag on it saying a member of the church Knitting Guild had made it and that it had been blessed by a priest at the church.

"I don't think it's been blessed," Will called to the church secretary.

"Well, you could take care of that real quick-like," she replied.

The priest placed his right hand on top of the red prayer shawl. "Lord, we give thanks for the gift of this prayer shawl. Bless it to the health and healing of Bessie Kilgore, as we give thanks for all her work for this thy Church and for the blessing of her presence among us." He hesitated for a moment. "Bless also the hands of your faithful servant who knitted this prayer shawl. We give thanks for her efforts and for her love of this ministry. In Christ's name, Amen."

"Amen," the church secretary replied softly.

"You know who made this one?" the priest asked her.

She initially shook her head no. "But it could have been that lady who sits over to the side of the nave on Sunday morning, on the left. You know that tall, skinny woman? She always seems so serious?"

The young priest nodded. "Yes. I know who you're talking about. Nan, I think's her name. I've never gotten a chance to talk to her."

The church secretary nodded. "I think she offered to help with the youth program once. It didn't seem to be a good fit, as I remember."

"Well, we all have our callings," the priest replied as he gathered up the prayer shawl and headed out the door. "Not everyone can minister to teenagers!"

"Ain't that the truth," the church secretary said with a chuckle.

She reached for one of the thank you notes she kept on hand. The church music minister had told her once that about half of his job consisted of writing thank you notes to parishioners. She took a blue pen and began to write a note to the lady who seemed so serious all the time. Maybe a nice thank you note would help her smile once in a while.

"Dear Nan, thank you so much for the gift of your time and talents to our Church! We appreciate you so very much. The prayer shawl you made has gone to a very special member of our parish who has given so much to us all. Have a blessed day."

Nan

When I picked the small note out of the mailbox, I couldn't imagine what it could be. The return address looked like the address of the church, though someone had hand-written it in blue ink.

I read the thank you note for my prayer shawl, and tears welled up in my eyes. Someone had noticed. Someone had appreciated my work.

I intentionally stayed as quiet as possible as I could at church. I hadn't volunteered for any committees. I hadn't volunteered to cook for any of the dinners or visit people in the nursing homes or go serve food to the homeless. The leader of my Inquirer's Class had once roped me into volunteering to chaperone a youth lock-in, but I spent the entire evening in a mild panic, shuddering with fear every time one of the boys threw a football perilously close to my forehead. I had never been so glad to go home and pick up my knitting needles and keep my own company.

That morning, exhausted though I was, I started another prayer shawl. It was what I could do. I'd never make an overseas missionary. I'd never be good at visiting people or cooking for people or working with children or teenagers. But I could knit for people. That's the one thing I could do and do pretty well.

I cast on a mere eight stitches with a cream-colored yarn, having in mind a triangular prayer shawl that would start small and grow until I ran out of yarn. I didn't have all that much of this yarn, so it would be a modest prayer shawl, a small prayer shawl.

As I knitted each stitch, I silently prayed.

"Lord, bless those whose lives are touched by this prayer shawl. Keep them safe. Give them peace. Help them to share their blessings with others."

Trip to Paris

Abby looked at the prayer list posted on the bulletin board of the church staff room, comparing it to the list of hospitalized parishioners the church secretary had just given her. Jill and Gary weren't on her list. They had called in this morning, asking for a visit from a priest, and the rector had asked her to make the call.

She took this job at All Saints after finding out about the food pantry the church ran. She figured this suburban parish might share her passion for ministering to the poor. She thought she might find something in common with her relief and development work. But here in Knoxville, she didn't have to worry about getting bit by mosquitoes and coming down with malaria. She had a real bed to sleep in and plenty to eat. She had air conditioning and a car to drive.

Working in a parish stateside felt overwhelming and even surreal at times. In her mission work overseas, she generally understood what challenges people faced. She made visits to their huts or chatted with them while they tended to their chickens or their goats. She listened as they told of their needs for the basics of water to nourish their crops, a cart to help get their crops to market, medicine when their kids got sick.

Here at home, though, people's problems were not so straightforward. People got upset. They cried during her visits. They stressed out over seemingly minor problems and looked to her for a listening ear, compassion, prayers, and even a way forward. Sometimes Abby wanted to shake them and explain to them that they had nice homes, enough to eat, and a bed to sleep in that wasn't on a dirt floor. What was their problem?

It took a "chat" with the bishop for Abby to lighten up and take her new parish problems seriously. Problems didn't need to be life threatening to cause anguish, the Bishop had told her. He asked her to listen to her parishioners in context, recognizing that all people, all over the world, had problems large and small. You didn't have to live in a third world country to have legitimate concerns, the bishop had said.

Abigail couldn't find Jill or Gary on any of the hospital or health concerns prayer lists. No one in the church office knew of any family discord, problems with children, or anything amiss at all within the family.

"So I guess I'll just go and see what they need," Abigail sighed. On the way out, she grabbed one of the prayer shawls she had just blessed. She would take it and leave it in her car. If the problem turned out to be something serious, she'd be prepared.

"I'm Abigail Mills, the new priest at All Saints. You asked for a pastoral care visit?"

A middle-aged man in a polo shirt and khakis ushered her into a spacious home in one of the more affluent suburbs of Knoxville. Abby followed him through a large entry hall, past a kitchen with a massive oven and granite countertops, then to the back of the house. A woman sat weeping on a cheerful yellow sofa. The man gestured for Abby to take a seat on an identical yellow sofa across from her, a glass coffee table separating them.

"My wife and I have had a bad time lately," Mr. Edmonds began. "Our daughter's in rehab, and she's only nineteen. Our older son is autistic, and Jill has had a hard time with him. It's a situation we worry about constantly."

Abigail nodded. Despite the luxury of their home – compared to her most recent field of ministry – this family had real pain.

"I'm Gary, by the way," the man reached out his hand to Abigail. When she took his hand, she felt the dampness of sweat on his palm.

"The thing is, we finally got Jill's sister and brother-in-law to take care of our son – and be on call for our daughter - for a week. I booked a trip to Paris – it's our twenty-fifth anniversary – and I hoped Jill could take a break from all this. But…."

"It's hard to leave, I'm sure," Abby said.

Jill nodded vigorously and began crying anew.

"Listen, I know it's not like a serious illness or anything. It's not like we're dying or have cancer or whatever, and I know flying off to Paris probably sounds like a cop-out…or just a good time. I guess some people would think we're so lucky, being able to take a trip like this. It's just that we're scared out of our minds that something will go wrong while we're gone."

"Sit tight," Abby told them.

Within minutes, she returned with a small, triangular, cream-colored prayer shawl. "I know this won't fix all your problems, but may I pray with you?"

Abigail draped the prayer shawl over Jill's shoulders and placed both hands firmly over Jill's head. Gary sat down beside his wife, his arm across her and the prayer shawl.

"We pray for peace. We pray for healing. We pray that Jill and Gary can have a period of Sabbath from their cares and their responsibilities. We pray that while they are away, their family will have good health. We pray for their protection, and we pray especially that You will guide and share Your peace with Jill's sister and brother-in-law. We pray that Jill and Gary might return with renewed strength to carry out their ministries to their children. In Christ's name, Amen."

Jill shook with tears. Gary wrapped both arms around his wife and wept quietly as he held her. Abby patted him on the shoulders and quietly left them. She thanked the Lord she had brought the prayer shawl with her.

Jill watched the sun rise over the horizon as the plane made its initial approach into Paris. She had worn the pretty cream-colored shawl during the entire flight. It kept her warm. It made her feel at peace with their decision to continue with their vacation, despite still feeling leery about leaving her sister with potential disaster at home.

The couple walked the streets of Paris, simply enjoying holding hands and taking in the sights and sounds of the city at a leisurely pace. They found a café down the street from their hotel, where they had a breakfast of baguettes, butter, strawberry preserves, and coffee each morning. They didn't speak during these mornings of bliss. They simply watched the early morning comings and goings of the city and rested their minds.

On the return trip, Jill kept the prayer shawl in her tote bag, taking it out to wear as their flight descended to their home airport. Gary clasped her hand, and she pulled the shawl tight around her shoulders.

"We can do this," she said to her husband before they disembarked.

"We can," he agreed.

As they entered their home, Jill's sister greeted them with hugs...before collapsing on the nearest chair in exhaustion. Jill took the cream-colored shawl and wrapped it around her sister.

Jill's sister kept the shawl and wore it regularly, before accidentally leaving it in a hotel on her own trip to Paris several months later. She had an early morning flight to make, and she thought she had packed it. She had, instead, left in on the bedspread of her hotel room, which was the same color as the prayer shawl.

The housekeeper of the hotel, an immigrant from the Democratic Republic of the Congo, found the prayer shawl and, since it was her last day on the job, took it with her. She wore it on her flight back home, thinking what a nice gift it would be for her grandmother.

Rogue Knitting Guild

"Actually, it's a spiritual discipline," Helen told the ladies gathered in common room of the Alderwood Assisted Living Center. She had arrived early to help the staff move the armchairs into a big circle before the twenty or so residents arrived. Helen brought cookies and punch. (She also had single serving sizes of pinot grigio hidden in her mega-sized knitting tote to share with the residents, a fact revealed only after the staff made sure the residents attending the meeting had settled in and had gone back to their regular duties.)

"What's a spiritual discipline?" an overly thin, balding woman croaked.

Helen hesitated. She had promised herself this rogue knitting guild would be for fun only. No religion. "It's something you do to make yourself feel better, like…meditating…or eating chocolate."

"Or partaking of holy spirits," gleefully chirped a full-figured, brown-haired woman who lived at Alderwood Assisted Living mostly to help take care of her husband. "I think those nurses have gone back to work," she added in a whisper.

Helen looked around behind her for any signs of lurking nurses and got up to pass around the wine boxes. "It's not like any of y'all are going to be driving this afternoon, is it?"

The mostly white-haired ladies chuckled and thanked Helen for the wine. It was hard getting alcohol delivered to this place. Even the grocery delivery services wanted a driver's license before taking an order, which many of the ladies didn't bother to renew any more.

"Okay, is everybody set with refreshments? Who needs knitting needles or yarn?" Three ladies, attending for the first time, raised their hands. Helen's self-appointed helpers, Barb and Nancy, brought out boxes of donated yarn and knitting needles for the new members. The meeting then devolved into cheerful conversation about proposed knitting projects, the upcoming dinner menu at the Alderwood dining room, along with any gossip anyone had managed to glean from any source at all.

Helen went around to make sure the new ladies had found skeins of yarn they liked and knitting needles to suit the yarn width. Barb and Nancy each sat down with a sub-group of women who looked like they were pushing ninety to untangle yarn skeins and frog hopelessly botched rows. The ninety-year olds sat back and enjoyed the attention. The younger women (those in their late seventies) knitted, mostly at a slow and peaceful pace, taking plenty of time to chat and nibble cookies.

At this point in the meetings, Helen felt free to step back and let the residents do what they wanted. Coming together was the point of it all. The only agenda items were to make sure everyone felt welcome, got a nice treat, attention, a listening ear from someone else in the group, and hopefully made a friend.

It all began when Helen had gone back to visit her former neighbor Harold St. Martin a second time at his studio apartment at the assisted living center. Harold had seemed even more surprised by Helen's second visit than her first. A visit by a former neighbor had delighted him the first time, but he had figured Helen had come for some sort of closure – or she missed his late wife or just plain felt guilty that he had moved here by himself and had virtually no one else who gave a damn about him anymore.

But that second knock on the door put him into a tailspin, wondering what she wanted from him. When she appeared, this time with a plate of cookies in tow, he actually thought about telling her he didn't feel well. But he let her in. Why not? It's not like he had anything else to do.

It was awkward. Helen had caught up on his life after moving to assisted living. She had dutifully told him how much she missed his wife, and they had shared a couple of stories of life back in the old neighborhood. Now what?

But the real reason Harold wasn't keen on letting Helen into his place was that he had given away that nice prayer shawl she had brought him. It wasn't that he didn't appreciate it. He did, very much. But he heard over dinner one night in the center's dining room that Ray Ogle, a man who lived around the corner, had discovered his cancer had come back. Ray had been moved to the nursing home section of the center. And everybody knew what that meant.

So Harold had taken Helen's prayer shawl over to his neighbor in the nursing home. Ray had slipped into a deep sleep – or maybe it was a coma – soon after Harold had arrived. He sat with the man for a few more minutes, then draped the prayer shawl over Ray's body, said a silent prayer for Ray's final journey, and left.

He didn't know how this would go over with Helen. But as she sat in the living room corner of his studio apartment, he knew she could see practically everything he still owned, and her prayer shawl wasn't there.

"Now Helen…I need to tell you something," he began.

Helen looked scared to death. She probably thought he was about to announce his own imminent death. Visitors here got spooked easily over that sort of thing.

"That pretty blanket, that prayer shawl you made me?"

"Yes?"

"Well, now I know you spent so much time on it and all. It was such a nice gift…."

Helen looked at him in severe consternation.

"It's just that I realized somebody here, one of my neighbors, needed it more."

Helen's face relaxed in deep relief. So did Harold's when he saw that she didn't look like she would kill him for giving away her knitting.

"But that's wonderful!"

"You think so?"

"I'm…well, I'm touched that you passed it on." Helen's eyes got all puffy, like she would start crying on him. Harold felt embarrassed.

"It seemed to be the thing to do. I don't think Ray even knew it was even there, to tell you the truth, but maybe he did. You just don't know at that stage of things."

Helen pulled herself together, much to Harold's relief. "Listen, here's the thing. I knit those things, but I never know who to give them to. You think there's other people here who could use a prayer shawl?"

Harold, at this moment, found a purpose for his new life in the assisted living center. "Yes ma'am, I do believe I could place just about any of those prayer shawls you bring me."

And he did. The problem was, Helen realized she needed help getting prayer shawls for Harold to hand out. He gave prayer shawls to residents moved to the nursing home unit, residents who lost their spouses or siblings or long-time friends, or residents who just plain got down in the dumps and needed a little perking up. Helen had never been the fastest knitter. She thought about asking some of the knitting guild members at church to help, but she didn't want her new project to get taken over by church bureaucracy. She didn't want to have to submit a budget or reports or get permission from anybody to do what she did. She just wanted to get prayer shawls handed out to anybody who seemed to need one.

Harold came up with the idea of helpers. "You know, I saw a gal looking over one of your prayer shawls in the dining room the other day. She asked what pattern you had used, what kind of yarn it was...like she knew something about it all. What was her name...Barb?"

Helen and Harold drew Barb into their conspiracy, then Barb brought in her best friend Nancy as well. Within a week, Nancy had gone around and gotten together a list of women who either already knew how to knit or wanted to learn. What Helen called The Rogue Knitting Guild (and which actually had no name at all) was born.

At first, Helen gladly provided all the yarn and knitting needles for the Rogue Knitting Guild. Some of the ladies had their own needles, but most didn't have cars anymore and couldn't get out to the craft store to pick out yarn. The money Helen used to put in the offering plate at church now went towards yarn and supplies. Helen enjoyed seeing her money put to immediate use and right in front of her eyes, giving the ladies at Alderwood a new hobby and a place to chat and make friends. As attendance shot up, Helen's friend Aggie pitched in to help with the costs. They made regular lunch dates to catch up with each other and then retreat to the craft store to choose yarns in all colors and weights to suit all the ladies who now attended the weekly knitting group.

The ladies usually knitted for an hour or so before deciding to head over to the dining room for dinner. Helen was always the last to go. As she gathered up yarn scraps and knitting needles for the group's stash, Harold slipped in to check on the how the group's meeting had gone.

"Mrs. Hillhouse and Mrs. G'fellers finished these prayers shawls," Helen told him. "And we should have some more by next week.

"Beautiful," Harold said, looking over the intricate stitching of the two finished prayer shawls. Helen had issued a perfunctory invitation for him to join the group, but he had gracefully and immediately declined. He was happy enough to get some of the other men in the center to help him make deliveries. Nancy had offered her services as someone with elegant handwriting to put a nice tag on each shawl, saying that it was a gift from the knitting group.

"Remember that first time I came to visit?" Helen asked as she closed up her box of yarn, ready to store until next week.

"I do," Harold told her. "Seems like a long time ago."

"I was scared to death," Helen told him.

Harold laughed. "I can't see you scared of anything."

Helen had to admit to herself that she was pretty tough. It had been hard to leave her church, but she had found herself and what the church would call "new ministry" here at the assisted living center. "I didn't know how you'd take one of your old neighbors showing up to give you some fluffy piece of knitting."

"I was scared to death you'd have a fit when I gave away that fluffy piece of knitting!"

Harold gave Helen a peck on the cheek before she left. Funny, how they'd become better friends now than at any time when he'd lived next door to her. You never knew what would happen in this life, even towards the end of it.

Helen waved and made her way back to her car. She'd be here soon enough, she knew. But she no longer dreaded the prospect of ageing to the point of needed assisted living care. Life, wherever it took you, was what you made of it.

A Shawl for Babushka

Ginger

"So you speak Russian?" the guy in charge asked me. His name was Robert, and somebody told me he had lost his job a few months ago.

I shook my head no. "Just a little." I hesitated to tell him more. Yes, I had been there, but it had been years ago. I wasn't sure tourist Russian counted, either.

"Anything will help, Ginger," he said. He gave me a clipboard and pointed to the check-in table of the food pantry run by the church.

I nodded and took a seat behind the desk. Glancing out the window, I could see thirty or so people already lined up outside to come in.

Steve walked by at his usual quick pace. "I'll be in the back," my husband told me. "You on greeter duty?"

"Yep. Robert thinks I can deal with all the non-English speakers."

Steve smirked. "Ginger, I know for a fact you can handle yourself just fine."

While Steve disappeared into the pantry office, doubtlessly to do what he did best – make deals on behalf of the pantry. Robert unlocked the door and let the first clients in to get some food. I put on my friendliest smile and asked for names and addresses. If someone didn't have an address, no problem. I knew exactly what that felt like.

We had settled into our new home in Knoxville nicely, but it hadn't been that long since we had lost our home in Houston. During the time we lived in a motel down the road from our flooded-out house, we didn't have a real permanent address, either. We had rebounded in the following months, mostly due to the kindness of strangers who had helped with everything from donated paper towels to hot meals served from a church trailer.

A skinny man who smelled of body odor approached my desk and gave me his name as Jimmy. He made small talk about looking forward to the good bread one of the grocery stores donated, telling me "I thank ye kindly" as he moved on to the long table of canned, frozen, and packaged food on offer for the day.

"Once wealthy, always blessed," Steve had said time and time again as we repeatedly found help from friends and family in the days after the hurricane hit. We had never had to sleep rough or go for more than a day without at least some kind of meal. Even in the days we couldn't even get close to our home, I still had some clothes. I didn't stink. Within weeks, I went back to a life with a bank account, a home, and stability.

These folks coming into the food pantry didn't have that going for them. I took their names and addresses. Fortunately, I didn't need information that might embarrass or intimidate them. The pantry had a policy of giving food to anyone who asked, regardless of what their story might be. I got that.

"Buenos Dias," I cheerfully greeted the numerous Hispanic men, women, and little kids who came through the line to get food. The pantry folks gave food to everyone. Immigration status didn't matter.

Robert had told me Russian-speaking folks occasionally went through the serving line. And sure enough, a family soon came up to my desk speaking a language I hadn't heard in many years.

A tall man with curly, light-brown hair stepped up to my desk and gave his name as Ruslan.

Memories of one of our more adventurous trips abroad popped into my head. Right after the Berlin Wall fell in 1989, Steve and I had ventured into the newly opened East Germany, taken unbelievably cheap train trips throughout Eastern Europe, and ended up in hotel in Moscow where no one spoke English. We had learned some basic Russian phrases by necessity, and I would never forget the sound of a Russian accent.

The curly-haired man looked surprised that I didn't ask him to repeat his name and could spell it. His wife murmured that her name was Natalia. Two stringy-haired, faded-blond little girls tried to hide behind the full skirt of an older woman who scolded them in non-stop Russian.

"Address?" I asked them.

"Knox-veeelle," the man answered.

"Okay, where in Knoxville?" I asked. Robert had told me they only asked for names and addresses to keep tabs on which neighborhoods or other cities clients came from, for grant writing purposes. But also, he told me, it also discouraged folks from going through the line twice…or more.

"*Ulitsa?*" I heard the Russian word for street come out of my mouth.

The man nodded. "Cleeench Av-uh-new," he told me.

"Clinch Avenue," I repeated. "You must live near the university.

The family simply stared at me. They would tell me no more, I knew. In their world, you didn't make small talk with strangers.

I watched the family move on to the food table. I heard the volunteers try to talk to them, to ask them what food they wanted, whether they wanted a frozen ham or a frozen turkey.

"No un-der-stand," I kept hearing in strong Russian accents.

I kept taking names and addresses from the steady stream of people coming up to the desk to get food. I wished I remembered more than the name for "street" in Russian. I wished I had gotten some sort of audio language course to brush up on words I might have remembered before I had started my shift.

"Need a break?" Robert came around to ask me.

"Sure," I said. One of the women I recognized from church, an older woman wearing a pair of jeans and an old but expensive looking blouse, took my station at the desk. I stretched and walked over to the back of the pantry, thinking I might find Steve.

I found him, but he had a cell phone pressed to his ear and paced the storage area. He gave me a quick nod and kept going. He had told me that morning he had gotten a line on buying cans of vegetables for the panty for ten cents on the dollar of the retail price. That would save the pantry thousands of dollars in food costs and make a great case for cash donations from the pantry's supporters. Steve disappeared into the office, the phone still pressed to his ear.

The cumulative body odor of our clients had gotten a little much for me. I stepped outside to a covered area on the side of the food pantry, where we offered day-old gourmet bread and week-old cut flowers from one of the pricey grocery stores in town. Over beside the street, the old Russian woman had sat down, head in her hands, with the little girls and their parents standing over her, looking anxious.

I went over to them, hoping to help and wishing again I had brushed up on my language skills. "Something wrong?" I asked. I had figured out on my journeys thirty years ago that tone of voice and body language went a long way, if you didn't speak the language.

"*Nyet, nyet,*" the tall man said.

"*Babushka* cry," one of the little girls told me shyly.

I crouched down beside the girl's grandmother and patted her back. I figured this whole scene was too much for her. Standing in line for food likely brought back some not-so-great memories, and I knew the language barrier could exasperate the best of us.

"It's okay," I told the grandma. "At least you have some food to eat. It may not be what you wanted, but it's something. You'll learn to ask for what you want. I promise."

The family likely didn't understand much of what I said, but I could tell, they knew I meant to be reassuring.

"Is there a problem here?" Robert had come through to check on the bread department.

"I'm not sure. They got plenty of food, but I don't think they knew enough English to get what they wanted. I heard the volunteers asking them to make choices; they just didn't understand the questions."

"You can't ask them what's wrong?" Robert looked concerned and frustrated himself.

"I'm sorry," I said. "I don't know the language well enough."

Robert watched in silence as I patted the babushka's shoulders and tried to convey reassurance, despite the language barrier. "I'll be right back," Robert said softly.

When he re-appeared, he had a prayer shawl over his arm - not one I had made, likely one his wife had knitted. He unfolded it and draped it around the grandmother's shoulders. She wept even more, but she raised her head and said many things in Russian to Robert. He nodded and patted her back. "I know, I know."

The family gathered up their groceries and began walking away. The babushka turned back, waving and speaking rapidly in Russian. I imagined she told us what she thought of her country, of our country, and what she thought of having to up and leave her home as an older adult who had never, ever expected to live in the United States of America.

We waved back. "Come back soon," I called. And meant it.

As I turned to go back to my post at the check-in desk, Steve raced past me. "That looked like that old lady who brought us dinner in that awful hotel in Moscow. Remember? When we couldn't find any restaurants open, and we paid the attendant at the end of the hall to find us something to eat?"

I nodded, remembering the beet and fish casserole the old woman had brought us. "That wasn't the best tasting food I've ever eaten, but it was the most appreciated food I've ever had. We would have gone hungry for a couple of days if she hadn't fed us."

I looked down the street at the old lady waddling behind her family. I did the math. "No, that woman would have been ninety years old by now. No way it's her."

"Maybe it's her daughter," Steve quipped as he dived back into the storage area.

"Maybe so," I said to no one in particular.

Maybe it was. Even if it wasn't, we had given back to someone from the country that had graciously hosted us years ago, even though we didn't speak the same language or have much in common at all. Truly, what goes around comes around.

I watched the prayer shawl on the back of the Russian grandmother. I thought of an old sweater I had left back in my closet in our farm house in Texas, a garment about the same color and texture as that prayer shawl.

That old sweater had surely molded, left in that closet above all that flood water. By now, someone had surely bulldozed our old house, including that sweater.

I watched the old woman disappear into a dented black car with mismatched hub caps, headed down a road back to a place she would never feel completely at home in. But for the graces of opportunities given to me, but for the kindnesses of strangers, I might have gone down that same road as well.

Blessing of the Cat Beds

Cassandra huffed down the side aisle of the nave as the parishioners arrived for the St. Francis Day Blessing of the Pets. Her daughter, Olivia, panned her phone across the row of colorful small blankets hanging across the altar rail. At Olivia's feet, a constant meowing sound emanated from an old plastic cat carrier.

"Another one peed the floor," Cassandra complained to Will and Abby as she stormed past them in the narthex. Each of the priests watched over their shoulders as the parish housekeeper marched down the hall towards her supply cabinet in the parish offices. Will hoped she wouldn't quit her job. As popular as the Blessing of the Pets was, he knew the event added "additional challenges" for the church staff.

As Will and Abby greeted incoming parishioners and their pets, Cassandra stormed back through with three rolls of paper towels and a garbage bag. Abby noted that Cassandra wore a dressy black skirt and floral blouse, rather than her usual grey cotton housekeeper's dress. Cassandra seemed unusually flustered. Abby hoped none of the dogs got loose this year.

"Now this year, we celebrate a new ministry," Will announced as the pet blessing got underway. "Thanks to our marvelous Prayer Shawl Ministry, All Saints Church has partnered with Knoxville's animal shelter to provide hand-knitted cat beds to all adoptable cats in the city."

Loud applause broke out. The rector smiled. He'd never guess that something as bizarre as cat beds would revitalize the yearly Blessings of the Pets service (not to mention bring a notable number of newcomers into the church), but he had learned long ago not to question the work of the Holy Spirit.

"What about the dogs?" a man in the back called out.

Many worshippers chuckled. "A ministry opportunity!" Will called back.

Abby shook her head, astounded once more that people flocked in to have their pets blessed and eagerly agreed to knit cat beds. Once again, she prayed for the wisdom to get a fraction of this number of people to work to end hunger in the community and think about what she considered more serious needs all around the world. But the bishop had given her a talking-to about that. She put on a smile and told herself to rejoice that this many people had turned up to a worship service at all. And really, she loved cats and dogs as much as anyone. In fact, she wouldn't mind getting a big golden retriever like the one sniffing the floor right in front of her.

"God separates the sheep from the goats, and today, we'll separate the dogs from the cats," Will announced. "Those with dogs, please line up to your right, and Abby will do the honors. Those with cats, we'll meet in the back."

As worshippers rose to corral dogs on leashes up to the front, Will made his way to the back of the nave. "Feel free to leave the cats in their carriers!" he called out hopefully.

The first several cats lined up for blessings belonged to parishioners who knew the drill and had wedged themselves to head of the line. Will sprinkled water on a grumpy old Persian cat, a thin tabby who looked like he had seen better days, and a limp spotted black and white cat who actually purred as Will said a quick prayer over her. Then came Cassandra, holding a small and feisty tortoiseshell cat.

Will looked at Cassandra with raised eyebrows. He had never heard her mention any pet around the office. Perhaps he needed to get to know his employees a bit better.

"Daughter's cat," she told him as if reading his mind. "This animal took that prayer shawl you left for me."

"Ah," Will replied. "God loves all creatures."

"She gave it to me, Father," the tall young woman beside Cassandra said, taking photographs with her phone without missing a beat. "Felicity took it. Look…" She held her phone out to Will.

Pictured on the phone, he saw a much mellower Felicity the Cat squinting at the camera, as if just awakening from a nice, long nap. He also noticed a big red heart under the photo with the number "496" beside it.

"What is that?" he asked.

"Oh, it's my social media feed. I'm uploading photos of all the cat beds and the pets. Hope you don't mind."

"This is Olivia, my daughter," Cassandra piped in. "She's always doing this social picture-taking stuff."

"It's my business, mom."

As Olivia took his photo while blessing Felicity the Cat, Will noticed out of the corner of his eye several people he'd never seen before come into the nave. They all had their phones out, pointing to the cats, the dogs, and the cat beds draped over the altar rail.

"I think some people saw my feed and came over to check this out," Olivia said.

"You have a business doing social media?" Will asked her, handing the cat back to Cassandra.

"Yep. And always accepting new clients...."

"Owwwwwwww!" screamed Cassandra. She held up her arm, deeply scratched.

"Mom! Don't let go!"

Too late. Felicity pushed off Cassandra's chest, leaped and landed on the Baptismal Font. Circling the narrow ledge of the font as the entire congregation turned to watch, Felicity dipped a paw into the water, shook it off, then leapt up to the choir loft.

"*Dios mio*," Cassandra gasped.

"Felicity, come here!" Olivia called. She did not look hopeful that her command would even be considered.

At that moment, Ginger's dog Gus saw the cat, broke loose of his leash and bounded down the aisle of the nave. "Ruff! Ruff!" he barked at the cat. Felicity replied with a snarl and a hiss.

"Olivia, get that animal out of this church!" Cassandra barked at her daughter.

"It's okay," Will told her. "These things happen." At this point of his rectorate, he had now seen it all. He stepped aside to bless the other cats lined up with their owners, carrying on as if bedlam broke out in his church every day.

"Olivia!" Cassandra pointed up to the choir loft and the cat, its back arched and ready to pounce on the dog, perched high above the entire gathering. "Get that animal out of here!" She marched out of the nave, pulling Oliva behind her and up the narrow staircase to the choir loft. Moments later, Olivia appeared behind the cat, camera in hand and filming the spectacle from a cat's eye view. Gus barked below, as Olivia slowly moved up behind the cat and swiftly grabbed her from behind.

Will saw his opportunity to gain back control of the worship service. "The Lord be with you!" he called out.

"And also with you," a good number of parishioners called back, after some shuffling and commenting on the latest churchwide drama.

"Let's all take our seats. If we're calm, maybe our pets will be, too."

He moved to the front of the nave and decided to pray while he had the momentum. He started at the far left end of the altar rail and silently prayed over each of the cat beds draped over the altar rail. By the time he reached the end of the row, the talking had ceased, and everyone had settled back into the pews.

Only one injury and no pets eaten by other pets – a successful Blessing of the Pets service, Will thought. He quickly blessed and dismissed the entire spectacle, nodding to the organist to start up the recessional.

As people and pets filed out of the church, Will and Abby noted the unusual number of newcomers who stopped to thank them for the service. "I wish I could bring my dog to church all the time," several of them said. Will responded with a jovial grin and quick laugh. This event had proved an unexpected success, but he didn't want to commit to a weekly hour of potential chaos without vestry endorsement.

Olivia and Cassandra hung back, waiting until all the church-goers had left. "I'm sorry, Father, for all the commotion," Olivia apologized to Will. Felicity the Cat looked equally remorseful.

"Not a problem," Will told her. "And could we talk about hiring you to help us out with social media?"

Cassandra sighed with relief. Maybe that prayer shawl had ended up where it needed to be after all.

Hats for Orphans

Tabitha called Abby as soon as she got off the phone with the adoption agency. "We've got a definite date to go meet our son in the orphanage!" she gushed as soon as Abby came on the line.

"That's wonderful! It's the little boy you told me about? The one in Eastern Europe?"

"Yes! We knew he was 'The One' as soon as we saw his sweet little face."

"I'm so happy for you," Abby told her. "Is there anything we at the church could do to help you get ready? I'll put you on the prayer list for sure...."

"Actually, the adoption agency asked us to bring donations."

"Oh?" Abby hoped she – or the church - wouldn't get hit up for a big cash donation. Lord knows the church had its own challenges with fundraising.

"They need hats. And scarves. And mittens, too."

Abby smiled. "We can totally do that. Are they for the kids in the baby home?"

"Yep," Tabitha replied. "It's the least we can do for the kids we can't take home with us."

"Of course. How many do they need?"

"A hundred sets. That's how many children are in the baby home. And they say they can only use cotton or wool."

Ouch, Abby thought. That would be tough. Or maybe not. "I'd like to introduce you to the Knitting Guild, Tabitha."

Abby met Tabitha at the door of the church to usher her into the Friday morning meeting of the Knitting Guild. New groups can be intimidating, Abby knew, and she wanted to make sure the guild members knew Tabitha's ministry project had the full support of the clergy.

"Ladies, we have a request for your labors of love," she told them after introducing Tabitha to the women she hadn't met. Melba and Martha had, of course, known Tabitha since her babyhood. "You want to tell us about the request you received?" she said, handing off the meeting to Tabitha. The ladies would take this better if it came from her.

"We're adopting a baby boy, and…."

Tabitha didn't get any farther, interrupted by gasps of joy and congratulations from everyone in the room. Martha got up to hug her, and Melba began planning a baby shower on the spot.

"That's not why's she's here," Abby told them. Getting church members to focus on something new always drove her crazy with frustration, but she remembered to remain persistent but patient. "The request from your adoption agency?"

Tabitha wiped little tears off her cheek. "A hundred babies and toddlers live in the same baby home – orphanage – as our little boy. And it's cold – very cold – almost all year round where they live. The orphanage staff likes to take the children outside for fresh air, even in the winter, but they want the kids bundled up hats, mittens, and scarves. They wrap them up pretty tight."

"So how can we help?" Melba took the bait and the lead. Abby relaxed. The project would succeed.

"They asked us to bring child and baby-sized hats, mittens, and scarves with us when we go to meet our son. The orphanage only gets minimal support from the government, and they depend on donations from adoptive parents – and their churches, or just people who want to help – to provide a lot of what they need for the children."

The faces of the women sobered. "They don't have warm clothes for the children, as far north as they are?" Melba inquired. Tabitha's joy had turned into a reality check for many of the knitting guild members.

Tabitha shook her head no. "They don't even have disposable diapers – or toys. Our adoption counselor said most of the toys we'd see in the baby home are American – they're all donations from adoptive parents."

"Count me in," Ginger Jordan said.

"Do we know these donations will actually get to the children who need them?" Jenny Lawson asked. As an attorney, she usually didn't have time to attend these meetings. Abby hoped she wouldn't put a damper on the group's enthusiasm for the project.

"I'll deliver them myself," Tabitha assured her. "We leave in a month to spend a week with our son, getting to know him and signing all the paperwork for the adoption. Even if I have to squeeze everything into vacuum bags, I'll get them there."

"You'll be fine travelling light – as far as your own clothes go," Ginger said. "Women over there wear their clothes several days in a row. Nobody will blink twice if you show up wearing the same thing every day."

"You've been there?" Martha asked.

"A long time ago," Ginger said. "Back around 1990. One of our adventures. Since we didn't have children, we travelled."

Abby noticed Tabitha look quizzically at Ginger, as if looking at a picture of what her life might have been. Or perhaps she realized she and this woman might have more in common than either would have guessed.

"My, that was before anybody went to the Eastern Bloc!" Martha looked at Ginger with new appreciation.

"Yeah, well, it was a different time." Ginger said as she fumbled with her knitting project, a hopelessly tangled cast-on row of a prayer shawl. "But the point is, you can live on very little there. You see the blingy lifestyles of the oligarchs on TV, but the truth is, almost everyone lives on just a few dollars a month – and in one-room apartments with a communal bathroom and kitchen at the end of the hall."

All the ladies stared at Ginger, hit with yet another reality check they didn't expect, and from a highly unexpected source, to boot.

"Let's get to work on this," Melba pronounced. "We have a month to get one hundred sets of hats, mittens, and scarves?"

Tabitha nodded. She shot a tiny smile of conspiratorial thanks to Ginger, glad that someone else at church appreciated that she didn't want just another over-the-top baby shower for her own child. She turned and smiled at Melba, too, glad that the group's leader had realized a need greater than planning a party for one of the church's own.

"Listen, girls, we need a plan. We can't just knit whatever we want and hope it comes out right." Martha had taken over the meeting, as Abby hoped she would.

"Why don't we divide up the work? Scarves are really easy, so maybe those who haven't been knitting for long could work on those?" Jenny suggested.

Abby nodded her assent. She reminded herself to contribute some knitted scarves, too.

"And those of us who done this since God was young can tackle the mittens," Melba added.

"I'll work on hats," Jenny offered. "I just made a bunch for my boyfriend's grandchildren. I can knock out one a day."

Melba's eyes widened at Jenny's acknowledgement that she was dating one of the recently widowed men in the parish. Church always provided drama and a steady source of gossip to those of them who lived fairly sheltered lives.

"I'll need somebody to help me," Jenny continued.

"Let me make some calls," Abby said. She had in mind some relatively inactive members who she knew knitted but had, so far, never participated in the knitting guild. This would be a good opportunity to try to draw them in.

"What about patterns? And colors?" Martha asked. "If the orphanage wants 'sets' of hats and such for each child, we need to co-ordinate."

"Do y'all know Clarissa…oh, I don't know her last name…she has that wild curly hair….You know who I'm talkin' about? That tall woman who always had such 'interesting' clothes. Isn't she an artist or something?

Abby inwardly chuckled. She'd soon find out if the parish ladies had figured out that their rector had a new girlfriend. "I believe she runs the women's center downtown," she said, hoping she wouldn't inadvertently let on too much knowledge of the situation.

"That's the one," Melba said. "Father Henderson brought her to Mrs. Tyson's Newcomer's Social. I met her then. We talked about art – I think she said she'd been an art major, before getting involved in the women's center."

"I believe you're right," Abby said. She made a mental note to alert Will Henderson that the word was out about his private life."

"Let's ask her to put together a color scheme for us," Melba announced. "I'm sure we could ask Father Henderson to invite her to work with us."

"Sounds like a plan," Abby said. She smiled at Tabitha. The meeting had gone even better than expected.

"Now Tabitha, honey," Martha asked over the top of her reading glasses, "when are you going to learn to knit? We'll need your help too."

"How about right now?" Tabitha said.

The Knitting Guild members all laughed in cheerful invitation. Melba reached into her box of donated yarn and needles to get Tabitha started on her first scarf project.

Connections

At the next meeting of the Knitting Guild, Jenny Lawson sat with the thin, leggy, and recently retired ballerina, coaching her through the basics of the stockinette stitch. Samantha picked up the knits and purls quickly. After all, Jenny realized, the girl was an expert in intricate movement. Of course, she could learn to knit like an expert in under an hour.

Up until recently, Jenny rarely attended the Knitting Guild meetings. Even though she had stepped aside from her law practice a few months before, she at least liked to think she had far more important things to do with her time than sit on her butt. But she enjoyed knitting. It gave her much needed quiet time – reflective time, honestly – after years of a too-busy mind and life.

She had become a regular at the weekly Knitting Guild meeting. One of the younger women, Tabitha Terrell, had asked her to help with a project to send sets of warm hats, mittens, and scarves to an orphanage for young children on the Arctic coast of Russia. That appealed to Jenny's sense of meaningful charity.

Following Jenny's suggestion, the group had divided the group into task forces to knit either hats requiring some knitting experience, mittens made by the most experienced knitters, or scarves made by the newbies (or, Jenny noticed, the older ladies who couldn't see very well any more). Jenny volunteered herself for the hat group. She didn't have the patience (or, quite frankly, the eyesight) for the tiny mittens. Long-time over-achiever that she was, she finished a small toddler hat during the first half of the meeting.

"Why don't you help Samantha with the purl stitch?" the deacon, Martha Craig, had suggested at one of the meetings. She said it as more of a gentle order than a suggestion.

Jenny got up and moved to the church parlor sofa to sit with the impossibly fit and toned ballerina she had met at the airport several months before. Samantha had come in late, shyly asking if she could learn to knit. Martha warmly invited her in and gotten her started with casting-on and the knit stitch. The girl wrapped her long, waist-length hair into a knot and got down to business, mastering the knit stitch within ten minutes. She sat with her legs folded criss-cross on the sofa, bending over to stretch every few minutes.

"I.T. band syndrome," she moaned in some sort of explanation.

The rest of the group nodded as if they understood. They didn't. The ballerina got back to work, saying nothing else until Martha sent Jenny over to help her learn to purl.

"So you're new in town? New to church?" Jenny asked after demonstrating the purl stitch.

The girl shook her head no. "Recently retired. I grew up here. I had to give up my ballet career in New York – my body can't handle it anymore."

Jenny chuckled. "Join the club. I'm retired, too. But you still have quite a few good years left in you. Many more than the rest of us!"

Samantha tried to smile. "I haven't figured out what to do with all those years. That's the problem with retiring at twenty-five."

"You'll figure it out," Jenny told her. "We all find ourselves in our thirties. You will, too."

By the end of the session, Samantha had finished about half of her first scarf. Jenny gave her a quick tutorial on binding off, so she could finish the scarf at home and get started on a second one on her own.

"Maybe I could start a hat next week?" Samantha asked.

Jenny hadn't intended to attend the meeting next week, but for this young woman, she would. She liked her and, for the first time in a long while, felt she could become something of a mentor to her. The young women who wanted to succeed in law always seemed so ambitious. They wanted advice on making partner, juggling motherhood with practicing law full time, or how to bring in the most lucrative clients. This young woman just wanted to figure out how to bounce back from an injury that had ended her beloved career and move onto a new one – a nice, wide open opportunity to explore.

"Sure," Jenny told her. "I'll teach you to connect two pieces of knitting next week. That's the only other thing you need to know to make hats – unless you want to work with circular needles."

"Sounds fun!" The ballerina dropped her project into a big shoulder bag and exited the room like a gazelle. The other women watched her with envy.

"Must be nice to be a size two and that tall," Martha said.

"Must be nice to be that young!" Melba added.

Jenny stayed until everyone but Martha had left, determined to finish tying up loose ends on the hat she'd made and turn it in as the first hat donated to the project for the orphanage. Martha stayed behind as well, tidying up the church parlor and picking loose strands of yarn off the carpet.

"Martha, got a minute?" The priest who led the Blessing of the Prayer Shawls service Jenny had attended poked his head in the room. He looked worried.

"What's up?" Martha replied.

The priest, Will, as Jenny remembered, cast a cautious glance towards Jenny. "It's a pastoral care thing," he told Martha.

"I'm comin'," Martha sighed. She left the remnants of the knitting guild projects and their iced tea glasses and followed Will out into the hall.

Jenny listened, though she figured she probably shouldn't. She could respect attorney-client privilege as well as anyone and felt a little aghast that the priest didn't do more than step out into the hall if he had a confidential matter to discuss with another member of the clergy. As she silently tied up her loose ends, she heard Will telling the deacon something about a staff member facing deportation – to Honduras, Jenny gathered.

"Oh no," she heard Martha say. "Has anybody called her daughter? She's a US citizen, you know. Won't that matter?"

At this point, the two clergy must have walked further down the hall. Jenny strained to hear them, but all she could hear was muffled voices that soon disappeared. The clergy entered the rector's office to finish their conversation, as well they should, Jenny thought.

She finished her hat, laid it prominently on the table where the guild always placed finished projects for donations, and paused to stretch her back after sitting for two hours. She started to pack up her knitting tote and purse, but she grudgingly decided to finish cleaning up the iced tea glasses, spoons, and napkins the group had left.

Servant leadership, the rector had preached at the last Sunday service Jenny had attended, about a month ago. Well, here was a service opportunity right here in front of her, and it wouldn't kill her to help out, Jenny told herself. She tossed all the crumpled napkins in the trash can and gathered up all the tea glasses and spoons onto a tray Martha had brought in from the church kitchen. Satisfied that the parlor was as clean as she could get it, Jenny hauled off the tray of glasses back to the kitchen in the basement of the church, loaded them into the industrial-sized dishwasher, rinsed the tray, and found where it belonged in the church's supply of serving pieces.

She walked back up the stairs to retrieve her purse and tote bag. Martha had not returned, and as Jenny walked through the church office area, she heard voices coming out of the rector's office. The entire staff had apparently left their posts for some sort of emergency meeting on the staff member's imminent deportment.

Jenny lingered in the church office on the pretense of looking over the various pamphlets and placards soliciting donations to worldwide relief efforts, participation in prayers for sundry situations, and appeals for help with the next churchwide dinner. She found herself wanting to do something, to make some connection with the church that she, so far, had not been able to make. Knitting the prayer shawls was such a solitary activity. Even if, as the priest had said over and over again, the prayer shawls meant so much to the people who received them, Jenny felt little actual involvement in what Will persistently called a "ministry."

"Jenny! I'm so glad I caught you before you left." Martha came out of the rector's office first, Will and the church secretary right behind her. "We're hoping to put together prayer support for Cassandra. We thought we should give her a prayer shawl. I gave her one a few months ago, but I found out she gave it to her daughter – always thinking of other people instead of herself."

"A prayer shawl?" Jenny looked at the clergy, dumbfounded at their response to what she saw as a serious legal matter. Life and death, even.

"I know it's a lot, but any chance you have one in progress you could finish up for her?"

"Listen," Jenny told the clergy, "you don't need a prayer shawl. You need a lawyer."

Jenny left her knitting bag beside the table of pamphlets and appeals for donations and corralled the clergy into a second impromptu meeting back in the rector's office.

Within the week, Jenny had formed a volunteer corps of retired lawyers ready to represent illegal immigrants threatened with deportation. She made lifelong friendships with these men and women and often met them for lunch, both to talk immigration law and for fun, too. Samantha, the retired ballerina who recently returned from a career in New York, helped the group with investigations and paperwork. She became a paralegal and now practices with a law firm specializing in immigration cases.

Jenny still knits when she has time – or when she needs a little breather from her busy retirement.

Mr. Fix-It

Will Henderson ushered the man into his office for a job interview. He winced at the man's smell, but it wasn't anything that a hot bath and a place to live wouldn't fix.

"Mighty glad to meet ya," the skinny man said, offering up a firm handshake.

"Come in, come in," Will gestured to the wingback chair across from his desk. "Robert tells me you worked a miracle over there at the food pantry, Jimmy."

"Well now, I reckon it just needed a couple a' three replacement parts," the job applicant sheepishly replied.

Will admired that old-fashioned kind of modesty. Jimmy reminded him of the people he used to meet at his grandmother's farm in Southwest Virginia, in the backwoods mountain country wedged between the Kentucky and Tennessee borders.

"What brought you to Knoxville?" Will asked. Robert had told him Jimmy lived rough downtown, turning up regularly at the church's food pantry. A polite man, Robert had come to rely on him whenever anything mechanical needed a repair. Jimmy had stepped in to fix an office chair he had seen Robert struggle to repair, quietly turning a few screws and bolts with his bare hands before handing it back to Robert. From then on, Robert found himself looking for Jimmy to come through the pantry's serving line every time the staff needed something repaired.

"Weren't no work to be had back home," Jimmy told Will. He looked down, embarrassed.

Will noticed and chided himself for not looking at the floor in embarrassment himself. In his younger days, he smoked. The day he knew he had given up smoking was a day he celebrated and looked back at with pride. He hadn't considered that giving up smoking – along with millions of other people – had also destroyed an entire economy that went back to colonial times.

"Tobacco farming?" Will asked.

"Yes, sir. All my life, up 'til a couple years back. It was mighty hard work, sweatin' and laborin' in the sun, but it paid mighty good. Then the gumment wouldn't give us no tobacco allotment no more…."

"But you're so good at mechanics. You couldn't find work in…I don't know…a factory, or something?"

Jimmy snorted. "Ain't no factories back home. No sir."

Will knew what he needed to do. "Listen, Jimmy," he said, dropping his southern accent a few notches. Folks like Jimmy trusted and worked with you better if you didn't come across as a self-important city boy. "We've got all kinds of landscapin' outside and maintenance work inside, and nobody to do it. Would you come to work with us and help us out?"

Jimmy grinned. "Well, now, I'd be proud to come to work fer ya, Mr. Henderson."

Will stood and offered a handshake. "Call me Will. And welcome to the staff of All Saints."

Two months later, Jimmy began his final Saturday afternoon sweeping before the Sunday morning church services. He had waxed all the floors in the Sunday School wing of the building, vacuumed all the offices, and tidied up the church gardens and flower beds. He always saved the sweeping of the entry hall and the worship space for last, making sure not a smidgeon of dirt or trash littered the floor before church the next morning.

As the summer sunshine shone through the windows of the entry hall, Jimmy reflected on how his life had made a turnaround. He had mentioned this to the reverend just that day, and the reverend had gone on about how death and resurrection were what the Christian faith was all about, after all. Jimmy took that to mean that generally speaking, life got worse and even hit rock bottom before it got better. And Lord knows, his life had done that.

He still missed the mountains of Southwest Virginia, the wild and steep ridges where a feller could find himself all alone with a huntin' rifle and a beer cooler, with nobody to bother him for miles around. He missed the little Methodist church his family had gone to, with the easy friendliness of folks he'd known all his life. He missed sittin' on his porch, knowing every car and who was in it as they passed by.

But workin' at this church weren't too bad, he'd reckon. The folks who came and went through here sometimes stopped to speak. Most of the time they didn't. That was fine by Jimmy, he reckoned. Most of them rich people acted like he was no more than a part of the building itself. Just meant he didn't have to try to talk to them folks. Some of 'em asked him to repeat what he said, like they didn't understand him. They'd all ask him where he was from, and not 'cause they were interested in him. More like they looked down on him like he weren't good enough to be part of their kind here at the church.

That's all right, Jimmy told himself. He didn't rightly know why he hadn't considered that he was "poor" before he'd come to Knoxville. He'd never thought like that back home. A few families had a little more than others back home. That was a fact. The Coxes had always had that rich bottom land along the Clinch River, and some of them had gone off to some fancy school, then moved away. He didn't see them folks again, unless they came back home to show off a big, fancy car or somethin' of that nature. But then they'd go off again and leave everybody back home the way they'd been all along.

Jimmy didn't know what to make of folks livin' rough in the city, under bridges and behind buildings, that sort of thing. He'd thought he'd come to town, get off at the bus station, look around for a job, and get a place to stay in a motel or some such. He'd come with enough money for that, or so he'd thought. But that money ran out real fast. Real fast. He'd ended up under that bridge with a big ole box to keep him warm within a week.

At that point, Jimmy thought he'd might as well freeze to death or starve to death in this big town. Nobody'd care much, he reckoned. It wasn't til that feller at the food pantry came up and gave him that red blanky that he decided that a few folks in this town did care about their fellow man. Only a few. It was enough, Jimmy told himself.

He finished up sweepin' and stretched his back, looking out onto the garden beside the church. He'd done all right, he thought. Work, a place to take a shower and wash up downstairs, an old pick-up truck the reverend had loaned him to sleep in – though he didn't let on to the reverend that he used it for that purpose.

"Hey, I'm lookin' to leave somethin' here for a donation," he heard a woman's voice call out from down the hall. He must have forgotten to lock the door to the Sunday School wing. He'd never heard of locking up a church building before he came to town.

A woman came towards him, two kids with her. She held up a big yeller blanket for him to see. "I want to give this blanket to the church," she said, yanking on a little boy with snot comin' out his nose. The little girl hid behind the woman, peeping out at Jimmy.

"Yes ma'am," he said. For once, he looked a visitor to the church straight in the eye. This gal didn't wear no fancy clothes. She talked like folks from back home, not like them rich ladies always comin' in wantin' him to step and fetch for them.

"I crocheted this blanket for the church to give to somebody," she said proudly. "I need to know where to leave it so as they can pass it on to somebody, like in the hospital or a nursin' home," she said.

"Why yes, ma'am." Jimmy stowed his broom and dust pan in a corner and wiped his hands off on his pants. "They put them blankets in this ole box in the office," he said, motioning for the woman and the kids to follow him. "They'll be mighty glad to get that purty thing," he added with a wink at her.

The woman beamed with pride. Her blanket looked fancier than the plain "prayer shawls" the church ladies brought in here. Jimmy liked it better, especially the yeller color of it. "Right-cher," he said, patting the side of the donation box.

The woman gave the blanket a little hug before gently placing it in the box. "Now they'll know it's here, won't they?"

"Yes, ma'am, I'll make sure the reverend hisself sees it first thing in the mornin'."

"Thank ya," she said, giving him a sweet smile. The boy had gotten loose and climbed on the cream-colored sofa Jimmy had just vacuumed. Jimmy figured that sofa had finally been put to good use. The little girl had found a flower vase on the reception desk and pulled out a flower to take with her.

"Y'all take some of them flaiyrs with ya'," he told her.

The woman looked Jimmy up and down, taking a good accounting of him. "Well now, that's right nice of you, sir."

Jimmy nodded, standing straight and tall as if he owned the place. "Now if there's anything else I can hep you with, you just let me know."

The woman jerked her son off the couch right as he began pulling a picture of Jesus off the wall. "Come on, kids. We need to get on back."

"Oh mom, I don't want to go back to that shelter tonight," the boy whined.

The woman turned her face so Jimmy couldn't see. "Come on, now," she told the kids. She jerked both up by the wrists and turned to leave the building.

"You come back, now," Jimmy called after her.

He retrieved his broom and pretended to sweep around the back door of the church as he watched the woman and her kids walk across the parking lot and get into a beat-up old Pontiac. The girl climbed over the front seat, pulling a pink, fuzzy-looking blanket up and over into the back seat with her. As the car passed by the door on the way out of the parking lot, the boy pressed his nose against the window and waved at Jimmy.

Jimmy waved back, and to his surprise, the good lookin' lady driving the car waved back.

"Anything else I can get you, Franny?" Robert asked his wife before heading off to the church's food pantry.

Fran groaned. "Uggghhhh. Help me sit up." He reached out to pull her up to sitting in their bed. She had just had her gallbladder removed the day before, and the four incisions in her abdomen hurt like hell.

"Crap, the door bell's ringing," Robert sighed.

"I'm not up to visitors," Fran told him as he sprinted downstairs.

But Fran brightened as soon as Will Henderson appeared at the door to the bedroom with a bright yellow blanket in tow.

"It's time you get a prayer shawl of your own," he told her.

Fran smiled. After all the prayer shawls she had knitted during the past year, she did appreciate receiving one of her own.

"This one looked different from all the rest. I hope it's not one you made yourself?" Will asked.

Fran fingered the stitches. "Nope. It's crocheted. Not in my skill set."

"May I?" Will gestured to the foot of the bed.

"Have a seat," Fran told him. "I may need you to pull me out of this bed before you leave."

Will laughed. "Tending the sick, it's what I do."

"So what's going on at All Saints? Tell me something good."

Will scratched his head. "Well, the big news going around the staff is that Jimmy – you know that guy I hired to help Cassandra with the heavy cleaning and the landscaping? – he's getting married. He told everybody yesterday morning."

"Who's the lucky girl?" Fran asked.

"That's the interesting part. She's one of the women living at the shelter. Clarissa said she's been there a couple of months, living with her two kids. She met Jimmy when she stopped by the church for some reason."

"Really? Do they have a place to live?"

"They do," Will told her. "Or will soon. You know Abby's lived in that little house next door to the church. After she announced she'd be going back to mission work, Jimmy came and asked if he could rent it. I'm embarrassed to say this, but he'd been living in his truck since coming to work at All Saints. Martha found him sleeping under a big red blanket, parked over by the playground, one morning."

Fran's eyes widened. She wondered if that "big red blanket" could possibly be the large red prayer shawl she had sent to the Food Pantry with Robert. "Jimmy was the guy Robert found at the pantry, the one who fixed the heat system over there? Rob called him 'Mr. Fix-It.'"

"Yes," Will said. "Mr. Fix-It. I like that. I'll have to start calling Jimmy that myself."

"So he's marrying a woman from Clarissa's shelter? Isn't that a little quick? With both of them homeless so recently?"

Will nodded. "They both needs homes, that's for sure. They both came to talk with me, together. They'd figured they could pay two hundred dollars rent between the two of them, with her working at a restaurant downtown and him working at the church. What could I say? Give shelter to the homeless – that's what it's all about – right?"

"Right." Fran pulled the yellow crocheted prayer shawl up around her. "I think it's time for another nap, Will."

Will squeezed her hand and closed his eyes. "Lord, I pray for Fran's rest and recuperation. I pray that she will find healing, improved health, and relief of her pain. In Christ's name, Amen."

"Amen," Fran replied. She yawned and snuggled down into her bed covers. "You can let yourself out, Will? I appreciate you coming over - and I love this prayer shawl."

"You're quite welcome, for both. I think Robert's still downstairs, I'll check in with him as I leave."

"Oh, what's the bride's name? The woman Jimmy's marrying? Maybe I'll knit a wedding prayer shawl for them."

"That would be nice," Will said. "Her name's Tonya."

Fran nodded as she closed her eyes to fall asleep. Why did that name ring a bell?

Last Rites

Will Henderson entered the hospital room gingerly, even though Aggie Claiborne had called to ask – no, order – him to attend Brickey Lane in his last hours on this earth. Tucked under his arm, Will carried the loveliest prayer shawl in the church's collection, a grey cashmere blanket with intricate cables and lacework. He also carried his well-used Bible and Book of Common Prayer. Sometime that afternoon, he would read the Litany at the Time of Death.

"Mrs. Lane? Helen?" He addressed the heavy-set, older woman with care. She had stormed out of a vestry meeting several months ago, never to return to church.

But at times like these, you put aside all the disagreements that inevitably arose in carrying out the church's work. When someone in the parish faced life or death, you conveniently put all that out of your mind and simply brought the love of Christ into the situation. That's what you did.

Helen took a breath upon seeing the rector of All Saints in the final hospital room of her husband. Her friend Aggie patted her hand, as if to reassure her that it was okay to allow the rector into this hallowed time and place, despite any differences they might have had, despite the fact that Helen had vowed never to attend All Saints again.

Aggie Claiborne still attended the Healing Service, the small and intimate service only a handful of the "oldtimers" attended each Wednesday at noon.

Though Will would sooner hide under his chair than call Aggie Claiborne an "oldtimer." In fact, she scared him. With her perfectly coifed grey beehive, tall and straight-as-a-stick posture, accentuated by a huge sapphire and diamond ring on her long, thin left ring finger, she was the kind of woman used to giving orders and expecting them followed immediately. Thus, he had hurried to the hospital to do his priestly duty as soon as he received her crisp telephone message.

"It's a difficult time for you, I know," Will began. "Mind if I sit?" he asked, pointing to a chair in the corner. Helen nodded, and Will relaxed.

"May I pray with you?" he asked.

Helen nodded again, tears welling up in her eyes. Will spread the prayer shawl over Brickey Lane's body. The man had already slipped into a coma, he reckoned, and had gone beyond registering anyone's presence. The death rattle had begun, and a nurse slipped in to hook up an oxygen mask to Brickey's face.

"Anything I can get you?" the nurse asked both the ladies and priest.

"We're fine," Aggie Claiborne answered for all of them.

The nurse looked familiar to Will. He glanced at her nametag, "JoAnn." Maybe she had attended All Saints at one time or another. He smiled as if he recognized her, just to be on the safe side.

Will rose to pray over Brickey. Helen and then Aggie joined him, reaching to touch Brickey's forehead all together in prayer. "Lord, we ask for your presence among us all. Cover your servant Brickey with your loving kindness just as this prayer shawl covers him with the prayers of his church family. Lead us this afternoon to know your love for us always. In Christ's name, Amen."

"Amen," Helen and Aggie said emphatically.

Will sighed with relief. It would be okay. The ladies had come home to the ministry of the church, even if just for this afternoon.

The nurse stepped inside to adjust the oxygen and check Brickey's vital signs.

"It won't be long, will it?" Helen asked her.

The nurse shook her head. "No ma'am. I don't think so."

Helen and Aggie sat down together as Helen's tears flowed down her cheek. Will opened his prayer book and placed it on the bed, ready for his part in leading the liturgy.

Relaxing into his chair as much as he could, Will felt oddly comfortable in his role. These ministrations to dying parishioners never bothered him as they might some people, even priests. In fact, he felt he was actually at his best in these situations – serving as a calm presence in the face of death, standing vigil, waiting out the process of going from an active life on earth to another realm of being.

Helen now rested in the arms of her friend Aggie, weeping softly. The two women were in their own world. Will closed his eyes to pray for Brickey and for his wife, friends, and loved ones.

Before leaving the office for the hospital, Will had popped into the knitting guild meeting at church to let them know about Brickey's condition. Melba and

Martha had gasped and told him how Brickey had been one of the founders of All Saints Church. Back in the day, even before the church building was finished, Brickey and Helen had hosted worship services in the spacious River Room of their home overlooking the Tennessee River. The children attended Sunday School in the solarium of the home, and Helen let them run up and down the staircase after the services while the adults enjoyed coffee and brunch.

Will sighed, thinking how sad it was that parishioners who had been such stalwarts in the church had come to leave it. He prayed for forgiveness for any role he might have had in the Lanes' disillusionment with his church. Maybe he should have stepped in more to advocate for Helen's plan to start a nursery school in the unused Sunday School rooms during the week. Maybe he should had tried harder to forge a solution to all the objections the other vestry members had with the nursery school plan. Tangling with the vestry often spelled the end of a job for a rector, but maybe he should had gotten tough with them nonetheless.

He thanked God for the gift of the Lanes and all their service to the church over the years. They had given their money, their time, and themselves to the church over the tenure of numerous rectors. All of his predecessors would have dropped everything to be at the hospital to be with the Lanes if this had happened years earlier. And that's what was expected of him, too. It didn't matter that the Lanes had a falling out with the church leadership, not in the end and not looking at the big picture of their tremendous contributions over the years.

When he opened his eyes, Aggie Claiborne had risen from her chair to pick up Will's prayer book and hand it to him. "I believe we're ready now, Father."

Will nodded and took the prayer book.

"Into your hands, O merciful Savior, we commend Your servant Bradford 'Brickey' Anderson Lane. Acknowledge, we humbly beseech you, a sheep of your own fold, a lamb of your own flock, a sinner of your own redeeming. Receive Brickey into the arms of your mercy, into the blessed rest of everlasting peace, and into the glorious company of the saints in light."

Will took a small vial of holy oil out of his coat pocket and made the sign of the cross on Brickey's forehead, anointing him with the oil. Helen leaned to kiss Brickey's cheek, then grasped his hand in her own.

Will continued as Aggie held Helen in her arms. "May his soul and the souls of all the departed, through the mercy of God, rest in peace. Amen."

The women whispered "Amen" as Brickey's breathing became more and more labored.

They waited.

Will rested his hands on Brickey's arm as Helen did the same on the other side of the hospital bed. As he silently prayed, Will's own eyes welled in tears. In that moment, he saw not only this man's death, but the death of the church as he knew it, the church he had grown up in and served as a priest. He saw the end of the Church Triumphant, the church that had changed the world.

As Will grasped Brickey Lane's arm, listening to his last breaths, he mourned the passing of a generation that had not only attended church with devout regularity but had also supported it financially through thick and thin. He mourned all those parishioners who would soon be gone. He mourned the power and glory of a full church building bursting with activity and passion for the work of the church.

Brickey took one last breath, and then was silent. Will felt a shiver run through his body, then a feeling of unworldly peace.

Helen let her tears flow freely, crumpling down onto Brickey's chest. Aggie stood aside, letting her friend have this last moment with her husband, and Will did the same. The nurse stepped inside the room and glanced towards Will, silently asking if she might begin her tasks.

Will motioned for her to step outside the room with him. "He went peacefully," he quietly whispered to the nurse.

JoAnn nodded. "I imagine she needs some time with him," she suggested.

"Yes, I think so," Will replied.

"You're the rector of All Saints, aren't you?" JoAnn asked.

"Yes," Will said. "I hate to embarrass myself, but do you attend All Saints?"

"Sporadically," the nurse told him. "I work most Sunday mornings. The last service I was able to get to was the Blessing of the Pets. What a fiasco."

Will smiled. "Bless you. I'm sorry the one service you could attend was so chaotic."

JoAnn laughed. "It was fun. I need a good laugh after working here so many hours. I'm just sorry I can't get to church as much as maybe I should."

"You're doing God's work right where you are," he told her.

Aggie leaned out of the hospital room. "I think Helen's ready to leave, Father."

Will nodded, and JoAnn followed him into the room. Helen had cleaned up her face and had her purse in hand, ready to go.

"Aggie's driving me home. I'll call you about arrangements, Father?"

"Of course." Will thanked the Lord for this moment of reconciliation. He had wanted to offer the church as a venue for Brickey's funeral, but he wasn't sure how such an offer would go over. "I'll keep the church schedule open. Whenever you feel like it, just let me know."

Helen nodded and let Aggie usher her out of the room and down the hall.

"I hope we'll see you at All Saints...some time," Will told the nurse. "But I understand if you can't make it. I meant what I said, you're doing plenty of ministry right here in the hospital."

"Thank you, Father Henderson," JoAnn replied. "I'd never thought of my job like that. I appreciate your understanding."

She went to take care of the body, glad to have had the chance to talk to the priest...and even more glad that she didn't have to feel so guilty for not attending church on Sunday morning. "Ministry, that's what I'm doing at this very minute," she said to herself as she pulled the grey cashmere prayer shawl off the bed and folded it neatly, saying a silent prayer of thanks for the priest's acknowledgement of her life's work.

Re-Use, Recycle

JoAnn

The family had left, leaving me with the body. I folded the prayer shawl Father Henderson had draped over the man, getting ready for the funeral home men. Wondering if the family might want it, I placed it over to the side, on a chair with the man's pajamas and a couple of magazines the family had brought for him before he became comatose.

It's hard knowing what to do for the families. They're all different. Some of them understand that their loved one is dying. They're prepared – or as prepared as they can be. They don't ask you to go above and beyond to save the patient. They don't make demands. They ask for comfort care.

Others never seem to get it until you have to tell them the patient has died. They see all the tubes and monitors, the blood tests and the EKG machines, and they figure we'll save the patient somehow. They keep asking the prognosis. Maybe they're in denial. Maybe they just don't know the stages of dying. A lot of people don't.

When the patient starts tugging at the sheets and can't get comfortable, it's time. There's not much we can do. Some dying patients claim to see loved ones who have already died. That freaks out some family members. I've seen it before.

I let the two dark-suited men from the funeral home in. They're always so well dressed. I suppose that's part of their job, looking respectful. I ducked out to let them do their job and shut the door behind them. We always try to shield the rest of the patients from this. I guess none of us wants to face this kind of outcome, even when the patient is an old man of eighty-one who died peacefully, as peacefully as it's possible to go. We should all wish to go as easily as this fine man. I think I even saw a little smile on his face, right before he went.

Thirty minutes later, I went back to clean the room. The grey prayer shawl was still on the chair, along with the magazines and the pajamas under it. The family hadn't come back. I don't blame them. They've got plans to make, people to call, grieving to do. I threw the magazines away and sent the pajamas to the laundry – maybe an indigent patient could use them. But the cashmere prayer shawl? I couldn't just throw it away, and the laundry wouldn't know what it was or what to do with it.

I ended up folding it into a tight bundle and stashed it away in the nurse's break room. Maybe someone else could use it – like the flower deliveries that charity made to patients who didn't get flowers delivered to them otherwise. It helped patients think somebody cared about them, even a stranger. Maybe it helped them feel better. You never knew.

"Nurse, could you do something to keep down the racket in the hall?" A frazzled, middle-aged woman with make-up long faded on her face after spending yet another night in her elderly mother's room came up to me at the nurse's station right after my shift started.

I leaned over the desk to see what the racket was. Two small children, maybe three or four years old, stood outside their father's door behind a make-shift barricade of chairs, singing off-key at the top of their lungs.

"Their father is very ill," I told the woman. "I'll see what I can do."

"Aren't children banned from this ward?" the woman asked, following me.

"I'm sure their mother brought them to see their dad. We usually don't let children up here, but the father really is very ill."

The woman frowned but didn't argue with me. Surely, she got my drift – the man in the room beside her mother's room was likely dying. Nobody but a complete ogre would begrudge him a last chance to see his kids. And the mother had enough to handle without trying to make two toddlers behave in a tough situation. The woman who had complained shut herself inside her mother's room with a firm whoosh of the door, leaving me to do the dirty work.

"Hey there," I said to the kids, a little girl with dirty-blond pigtails and a little boy with a buzz cut. "We need to be quiet," I whispered to them.

I looked inside the room. The wife, twenty-something years old and wearing a blue t-shirt and jeans, sat beside her husband, holding his hand. She wept. He looked dejected. I hoped he would bounce back. I hoped the new antibiotics we had given him would kick in and bring him back. But it didn't look good.

"Anything I can get you?" I asked.

The wife shook her head no. The kids, barely contained behind the chairs blocking the door to the hallway, started up with their singing again. The patient turned his head away from the noise. The kids' racket probably bothered him, but he didn't want to say so. At least that's what I thought. The wife seemed to have given up, too. She wasn't up to disciplining her children.

I needed to do something. The woman who had complained was in the right. Children weren't allowed here. We bent the rules from time to time, but when they bothered other patients and somebody complained, we had to put the foot down.

My own kids wouldn't have behaved much better at that age. When you took them someplace where they needed to be quiet – like church, the doctor's waiting room, that kind of thing – the trick was to give them something to play with that would distract them from their own boredom. Otherwise, they'd act out and make everyone else miserable.

I turned to the kids. "Listen, I want y'all to be as quiet as you can. I'm going to see if I can get you some prizes. But you need to be quiet if you want one. Got it?"

The children stared at me. But they calmed down and watched me climb over the chairs and go down the hall to the break room. I looked back, making a shushing gesture before disappearing from their sight.

The break room was empty. I had hoped Jennifer, one of the nurses working part time after maternity leave, would be around to possibly lend me some baby toys she likely had in her purse. Most moms of little kids usually had at least one or two toys packed up in reserve for situations like this.

What could I use? I'd have to improvise. It's what nurses did at times like this. I grabbed the grey prayer shawl from off the shelf where I'd left it earlier. Looking around for possible substitute toys, I also grabbed a stack of plastic cups and a fistful of plastic spoons. I couldn't take anything small; the last thing I needed was a choking hazard. I took an armful of magazines that looked relatively clean and a box of napkins.

"Look kids!" I called to the kids. They stood behind their barricade, relatively calm and watching for me to reappear.

I climbed over the chairs and looked over to the children's parents. The wife had buried her head onto her husband's chest, shaking with grief. They likely didn't know I was there.

"We're going to have a pretend picnic," I whispered to the kids." I unfolded the prayer shawl and spread it out on the cold tile floor of the hospital room. The children looked up at me wide-eyed, as if a pretend game like this was something they hadn't done on a regular basis, if ever. I was sure the ill father had taken up most of the mom's time and attention.

I pulled out the magazines, which mercifully featured lots of recipes. We nurses were always trading recipes and gabbing about what we'd like to cook, even though we usually just ordered in when we got home, too exhausted to lift a fork, much less a skillet.

"Let's pretend this is the food," I said to the kids, flipping through the magazine until I found a two-page spread of a Thanksgiving turkey with all the fixings. I tore out the pages and put them in the middle of the prayer shawl, now re-purposed as a pretend picnic blanket. "And make sure everybody has something to drink." I handed out cups, putting out extras for any pretend people who might join us.

The little girl gingerly picked up two cups and mimed pouring one into the other. The little boy grabbed the magazine and pulled out pictures of new cars. That worked, I decided. At least they weren't out in the hall yelling. I helped the little girl "fill" all the cups and "set the table" with all the spoons. As she started passing out the napkins, I stood up and backed off their play.

I checked the patient's pulse and took a glance at his monitors. No change. The wife had nodded off on her husband's chest, no doubt exhausted from this long process. Maybe it would be over soon, for better or for worse.

Before I left, I took a look at the children's play supplies. They played contently on the prayer shawl. The little boy had rolled up the edges to turn the prayer shawl into a big comfy nest for himself and his sister. They didn't even notice when I ducked out of the room.

Two hours later, the children's grandmother arrived to take them home – or probably her own home, I guessed. The patient's wife came out to give them hugs and kisses. She seemed relieved for them to go. I wondered if maybe we should have told her the kids were far too young to visit. But she was so insistent that they see their father – at least one more time. In any case, all of them seemed glad when Granny showed up to whisk the kids away.

The chaos started up again as the family packed up the kids to go home. The woman in her mother's room next door stuck her head out the door to grimace at them.

"They're leaving." I told her. She nodded and shut herself back inside her mother's room.

"We goin' to Gan-Gan's house!" the little boy announced as I stepped inside his father's room.

"That's great!" I said. The little girl ran up to me for a hug. The wife gave me as much of a smile as she could. I could tell she appreciated the play equipment I'd set up.

I watched the Grandmother and the two kids make their way down the hall towards the elevator. The little boy dragged the grey prayer shawl behind him.

I stepped over to the nursing station and asked the secretary, "did the family of Mr. Lane come back for his things?"

The secretary nodded no. "I asked if they wanted us to hold anything for them. They said no."

I turned to watch the grandmother and my patient's kids, catching a glimpse of them right as the elevator doors closed. The little boy had the prayer shawl draped over his shoulders like a superhero's cape, waving to me as the doors closed shut.

I waved, thinking what a roller coaster day that lovely grey prayer shawl had had.

Wine and Bread at the River

"A perfect day," Will Henderson declared as he and Clarissa sat down on the big blue and white checked knitted blanket beside the Tennessee River. He had picked the place, the sprawling public park running alongside the river a few blocks from the church. The city kept the grass mowed down to a pleasant carpet of green, dotted with leafy mature trees providing just enough shade for a private picnic.

Clarissa chose the menu and insisted on preparing everything herself. Will appreciated having someone prepare a meal for him again. He had burned out on take-out junk food and bland frozen dinners within weeks after his ex-wife left. He knew he should have offered to bring something, but by this time in their relationship, he knew and Clarissa knew that even a simple lunch was beyond him.

Will watched Clarissa intently as she carefully unpacked a willow picnic hamper. Pulling out a lovely cream-colored ceramic plate with a colorful butterfly pattern, she laid it out between them, followed by the placement of a round loaf of crisp bread.

"I thought we'd share," she said, briefly glancing up to gauge his reaction.

He smiled back, noting that she looked as if she were setting out the large round loaf of bread for celebration of the Holy Eucharist.

She lifted two clear plastic wine glasses out of the hamper, along with a bottle of chardonnay. "Want to do the honors?" she asked, offering him the bottle and a corkscrew.

He pulled the cork for her as she set out chicken salad, melon slices, and oatmeal cookies. A slight breeze blew their hair askew. He watched as she pressed her wayward blond curls out of her face. And what a lovely face it was, he thought.

Clarissa broke the bread in half and offered Will a chunk. As he took it, he caught himself staring into her eyes, captivated by the inner joy and the deep strength he saw within her.

"You know, you're more of a priest than I am sometimes."

Clarissa rolled her eyes. "What in the world makes you say that?"

Will thought for a moment. His observation had simply blurted out. "I see you doing so much good in the world. What you do at the women's center every day makes such a difference. I wish I had that."

Clarissa regarded him with raised eyebrows. "You don't think what you do makes a difference? That's a hell of a thing for a priest to say."

"Yeah." Will helped himself to the chicken salad, spooning a heaping portion onto a chunk of bread. "Yeah, I guess it is."

"But that's how you feel? Are you burning out on the priesthood thing?"

Will grimaced. For not the first time, something about Clarissa made him say exactly what he thought. "I guess I am."

"Hm," she replied.

"That's all? You're not shocked?" he asked.

She shrugged. "Priests are just as human as the rest of us. You don't think you're immune from burnout?" She picked up a piece of melon to eat.

Will couldn't help thinking about all the talk in seminary about how priests were "set apart" by God for divine duties. "No, I'm not immune from burnout. I suppose I'm ripe for it, after the divorce and all."

"Time to move on?" She leaned back on her elbows and watched his face intently.

He looked into her eyes. "Yes. Absolutely. Time to move on."

Her lips smiled a slight smirk. He knew and she knew what she had really asked. Was he ready to move into a new relationship? With her? Yes, that was the answer to both the asked and unasked questions.

"So. What next?"

He wanted to kiss her. But not yet. Get the other stuff out of the way. "I think I need to deal with the burnout head-on. I think I need to discern where I need to go, what I need to do."

She nodded. He could tell she understood what he meant, that if he felt called to move away, to follow another call to another ministry, that he would need to do that before their own relationship could move forward.

"What is it you do best?" she asked. "Is there anything at all about being a priest that still gives you joy?" She used the people skills she used professionally with the broken souls she helped on a daily basis. He knew that and nodded. He could use her help in figuring out what to do with his ministry, and it was okay to accept her help. Lord knows she was one of the few people currently in his life he could confide in.

"This is going to sound creepy, but I do well with the old people. The ones close to death. The ones needing – and welcoming – someone to help them make that transition to the next life. The ones who know they're dying but still fighting it. I offer them companionship on that journey, and they let me go with them…well, as far as I can."

Clarissa nodded. Will sighed in relief. She didn't think him creepy or crazy or even weird. She got it.

"And with all the old people in church now, there's a lot of that to do."

Will nodded. "Yep. And dwindling finances to fund it all."

"The church is dying, too."

Will hesitated. "Yes, it's not the same as it used to be."

"So maybe you need to be there for the church itself. As it transitions to the next stage…whatever that is."

Will stared at her. Of course. Why hadn't he made this connection before? Watching the church age, watching the once vibrant ministries slowly but surely fail to work – it was exactly like watching an elderly person wind down, sometimes fighting and angry about the changes. And he helped the elderly find peace. He helped the elderly know that it would all be okay, that God would not abandon them even unto death.

"Yes. That's my ministry. Ushering the church into its last years, walking with it as it winds down, helping it resurrect and transform into something new."

Clarissa smiled. "Well, that was quick."

Will snorted. "You're pretty good at pointing people in the right direction, you know."

Clarissa popped a cookie into her mouth. "It's what I do," she quipped.

She offered a cookie to him. He leaned forward and met her lips with his own, pressing into her, enjoying her, communing with her beautiful essence.

They looked each other in the eyes, close up. "So I guess we're moving forward, huh?"

"Guess so," he said.

The wind blew her hair into his face, and he reached to caress her face. The sun shone bright and warm onto the handknit blanket. The river water sparkled like a sea of white diamonds.

A perfect day, indeed.

Adoptive Mother-To-Be

Tabitha

I held in my hands – ready to be blessed – my first baby blanket for my precious baby boy. I had worked hard on this blanket, using a delicate lacy pattern with tiny size three needles. Finally, I had finished.

I waited for the priest to call for new prayer shawls to be brought to the altar for the Blessings of the Prayer Shawls ceremony. I wouldn't – couldn't – leave my precious baby blanket up there before the service, fearing someone might pick it up and give it to someone else by mistake.

We had met our new son three months before, in an orphanage four thousand miles away. The moment I saw him, I knew he was mine. He was small for his age and malnourished, bundled up in three layers of clothes and capped off with a blue cotton baby hat. He looked at me with his hazel eyes and pointy little nose. Finally, I had a child.

My husband plucked the blue baby cap off his head, revealing soft brown hair. The orphanage staff, satisfied as we cooed and hugged our new son, left us alone to get to know him. I spread my coat out on the floor of the orphanage, and we sat our son down on top of it to crawl and play with the small toys we had brought with us all across the ocean.

We both walked him around and around, holding our baby tight in our arms. It was what he needed. As one of ten infants in his group of babies, he wouldn't get enough hugs, enough love, he needed to thrive, despite the best efforts of the three dedicated caretakers of his group.

It took hours and lots of attempts to hold our new son's eye contact, but we eventually got our son to smile. Slowly but surely, he got comfortable with us.

When the orphanage director came to get him at the end of the morning, our son whimpered and began crying when she took him away from us. I knew that was a good sign – he had begun bonding with us – but I wanted to take him back into my arms and hug him until the end of time.

Leaving him there was the hardest thing we had ever done. The country of his birth required us to make one trip to meet him, finalize all the paperwork, then return months later for our court date to make him ours.

The night before we left on this first trip, my husband and I both awoke before dawn, realizing we would have to leave the country without our son. We both cried and cried with the most profound, raw grief I had ever felt, holding onto each other in the pre-dawn light of a land where we would have to leave our new son behind us.

When I got home, I knitted even more than I had before, trying to cope with the anxiety and pain of our separation from our new son. This time, instead of making garments for unknown and multiple children, I knitted hats, rompers, and sweaters for my own child.

I soon had more than he could ever wear in one season, so I knitted warm scarves as gifts for the orphanage staff. I knitted and knitted and knitted, sometimes into the wee hours of the night, trying not to lose my sanity while waiting for the call to return and become my son's mother for good.

The weekly meeting of the church Knitting Guild became my support group, and one I desperately needed. The ladies in the group, now my friends, asked each week if we had heard anything from our adoption agency. They asked how we were holding up. They prayed for us, for our son, and for all the children and caretakers in the orphanage each week. They started a new batch of summer weight sweaters and rompers for me to take back to the orphanage with me.

"Why don't you knit a prayer shawl for your baby?" the deacon asked as I packed up to leave one of our meetings.

"We thought about making one for you," the deacon continued, "but a prayer shawl for someone you know is so personal. We all felt you'd want to make the prayer shawl for your own son yourself."

I started a prayer shawl for my son, something special that no one else in the world would make for him. I purchased soft baby-blue yarn, a cashmere blend, and found a pattern that would keep my hands busy and my attention off my worries and fears. Since the pattern required small needles, it would take me a long time to knit. Just what I needed.

And I found myself praying as I knitted this intricate baby blue blanket. I prayed for my son. I prayed that he would stay healthy, that he would stay safe. I prayed that his caretakers would pick him up as much as they could and that they would cuddle him and hug him as if he were their own. I prayed he would have toys to engage his mind. I prayed the orphanage would find enough food for him to eat. I prayed for him to get milk.

In the wee hours of the morning, I imagined sending my prayers, my soul, my body, thousands of miles away to his crib in the orphanage. I imagined my love surrounding him, enveloping him, floating all around him in a cloud. I whispered to him that I loved him more than anyone else in the world. I told him that soon, very soon, I would be there to hold him in my arms again. I would be there to take him home for good.

I prayed these thoughts every night in my own bed. I prayed these thoughts every time I feared I would never see my son again. I prayed these thoughts every time I took up my needles to knit for him.

Finally, we got the call. We would leave in three weeks' time. We had a court date. We booked the plane tickets. My hands shook constantly, hoping and praying everything would work out, that we wouldn't have last minute glitches or that in some awful unknown way we would lose our precious boy.

I finished my baby's prayer shawl two days before we left to pick up our son. As the priest blessed my prayer shawl, I felt a confident peace and assurance that we would get back to the orphanage, get through the court hearing, officially become my son's parents, and bring him home. "Amen," I said firmly as the priest who had helped shepherd us through the long process released her hands from my prayer shawl.

My son had grown from a baby to a young toddler when we returned to the baby home. I opened my arms when the orphanage director brought him to us. I wrapped him up with my prayer shawl. I wrapped him up with my love, and my husband wrapped himself around both of us.

Every stitch, every prayer, I had knit on this long journey had ended here. My son looked up at us, began to look away, then looked back into my eyes in recognition with a perfect double take. "He remembers us!"

We dressed our new son in one of the hats and baby outfits I had knitted long ago. We wrapped him in a cotton blanket for warmth and in the prayer shawl for love. After saying our goodbyes and thanks to the orphanage caretakers that had cared for my son as best they could – giving each of them a new hand-knitted scarf – we stepped outside the orphanage for our long trip home, into a new life for all of three of us.

Mrs. Tyson's Last Baptism

Mrs. Tyson ascended the elevator she had paid for herself, arriving late to the Sunday morning service and baptism. She had shooed off her caregiver, firmly suggesting the woman go for a long coffee break. She wanted to be alone for what would likely be the last baptism she would ever attend.

Her niece, Tabitha, had just arrived back from Eastern Europe with her husband and a baby boy they'd adopted. Mrs. Tyson had sent over a hand-knitted baby blanket her own mother had knitted for all her children's baptisms, way back eighty-some years ago. Having had no children herself, Mrs. Tyson had passed it on to Tabitha, and the baby blanket finally had come out of its careful wrappings for its first use in the twenty-first century.

How odd, Mrs. Tyson thought, that her mother's knitting would end up swaddling a baby born so far away, connected by nothing but the work of the Holy Spirit. As Mrs. Tyson's wheelchair glided out onto the second floor of the church and through the automatic doors to the choir loft, the assembled congregation was just finishing the last strains of "Lift High the Cross," Mrs. Tyson's favorite hymn. She wheeled down the gently sloped ramp she had also paid for, taking a place right up against the railing at the front of the choir loft, so she could look down upon everyone and everything in the church.

A full house, Mrs. Tyson noted with satisfaction. Most of the pews filled, the clergy wearing their white robes, the church banners lifted by the young acolytes, and the mighty beams holding up the roof pointing towards heaven, ringing with the music from below. Mrs. Tyson reminded herself that all things really did work together for good. Her caretaker's delay in getting the car pulled around for their departure had resulted in her arrival at just the perfect moment.

"The Lord Be With You!" Father Henderson called out.

"And Also With You," the congregation responded.

As he read the opening prayer, Father Henderson looked up to the choir loft and caught Mrs. Tyson's eye. He gave her a slight smile as he continued his prayer, and she gave him a subtle wave. No one else would see her, she knew. That's why she had paid for an elevator, paid for a ramp down to this very spot. She had so enjoyed watching church services from the choir loft as a small girl, peeping over the rail as her mother sang in the choir and her own father preached down below. She loved seeing behind the scenes of the service, whether the parishioners below whispered during the sermon or ducked out early. She remembered waiting with her mother to receive Holy Communion, trooping down the small staircase from the balcony, holding her mother's hand to rush in and be among the last to kneel down for the sacrament.

Tabitha and her new family moved to their places at the front of the nave. Will read the timeless words of the baptismal service, asking Tabitha and her husband to renounce evil and bring up their new child in the light of Christ.

Mrs. Tyson noted a twinge of sadness in Will's face. He still seemed restless. Even though he had proposed to Clarissa and had begun making plans for their wedding, she wondered if this might be his last baptism in this place as well. The last time Will had visited, he confessed that he had found himself on another diocese's shortlist for a new bishop. He humbly waved off any possibility that he would be chosen, but still, he seemed open to a new call of some sort.

"You know, deep down, when it's time to go," she had counseled him.

The priests, Tabitha's family, and the acolytes now paraded to the baptismal font at the back of the nave. Father Henderson motioned for the young female priest, Abby, to lead the next part of the service. The young woman looked happy for once, Mrs. Tyson noted. She'd worried that her church wasn't quite the right fit for this new priest, and sure enough, the young woman had discerned that parish ministry was not for her. She'd be leaving soon. But she said she'd learned lots during her time at All Saints. Mrs. Tyson accepted that, appreciated that.

Tabitha lifted the white knitted baby blanket away from her son's face, exposing his nearly bald head. She handed the child to Abby as a member of the altar guild handed Will a large silver pitcher of water. Abby scooped three handfuls of water over the baby, baptizing him in the name of the Father, the Son, and the Holy Spirit. His name was John Tyson Terrell, a choice that both pleased and deeply touched Mrs. Tyson. The Gospel of John had always spoken to her in its mysticism, and the boy's middle name was a lovely tribute to her husband's family, who now had no living offspring.

The baby wailed, the congregation chuckled, and Tabitha, beaming, wrapped the white blanket around her son's head to keep him warm and dry. Father Henderson asked to hold the child, walking up and down the middle aisle of the church to introduce him as the newest member of the Body of Christ.

Mrs. Tyson watched the faces of the parishioners as Father Henderson showed off the infant. The new couple, the ones from Houston who helped out so much with the food pantry and who had comported themselves so graciously at her newcomer's social, watched the baby with amusement and perhaps a little sadness. They had no children, they had told Mrs. Tyson. She knew how that felt and admired the greying red-haired woman's spunk, despite the sadness she must have overcome.

The quiet lady, the skinny woman with the thin ponytail who always wore the same tired shirtdresses and no make-up, closed her eyes as if in prayer. Mrs. Tyson wished she had gotten to know the woman better. She attended every service, pledged a small amount paid on time every single week, and – according to Father Henderson – donated a new prayer shawl to the church at least once a month. The woman seemed so pious, much more pious than Mrs. Tyson could ever hope to be. But we all have our gifts, Mrs. Tyson reminded herself.

The woman who had gotten that volunteer legal aid group started smiled broadly at the baby as Father Henderson walked by her, midway down his march down the center aisle. A tall and very slender young woman sat beside her. They whispered to each other during the prayers. Despite the age difference, they seemed to be good friends.

Robert, the man who had recently taken over administration of the food pantry, looked at his watch. Mrs. Tyson remembered that he had proposed opening a new branch of the food pantry to serve the low-income neighbors of the church right after the service. His wife, Franny, wearing a bright pink dress and matching glasses, waved to the baby as he passed beside her.

After the baptism, Mrs. Tyson wheeled her chair around to leave. Father Henderson had embarked on a sermon about hope and new life. Mrs. Tyson had heard it all before. His words would make no difference now. A choir member bent towards her to ask if she were all right. She waved off the choir member, telling him she was fine.

Really, she wanted some time alone in this building that had meant so much to her. She wanted to roll down the hallways of the Sunday school rooms where she had muddled through as a teacher decades ago. She wanted to look out onto the courtyard she and her friends had planted with flowers and azaleas back in their days as young married women of the parish. She wanted to pause beside the cozy church library where she had sought solace and answers so many times within its paneled walls and ceiling-high bookcases.

Mrs. Tyson rolled up beside Father Henderson's empty office and stopped. The rector had gone through a bad patch himself, often coming to see her and staying at her home for an hour or more, in despair over his failed marriage. She had done nothing more than listen, but this seemed to have been enough. We all need someone to listen to our troubles, even if we can't fix them, Mrs. Tyson knew.

The eccentric woman the rector had brought to the newcomer's social had surprised her. Upon first appearance, Mrs. Tyson had assumed the rector had brought in a refugee from the women's shelter the church supported. But the curly-headed woman with the colorful clothes had turned out to be the director of the women's shelter – and also the woman who had knitted her own beloved prayer shawl in shades of yellow and cream, soon to be Will's wife.

Mrs. Tyson, in fact, had brought the prayer shawl with her. It had slipped down behind her, wedged in between her body and her wheelchair. She reached to pull the prayer shawl up onto her shoulders. As she did, unseen hands helped her, pulling the prayer shawl up and over her shoulders. The church housekeeper, a middle-aged Latina woman, made sure the prayer shawl was tucked securely over her chest and stepped back to ask if she needed something.

"You need a glass of water? You need me to call somebody for you?"

"I'm just fine, dear. Just fine," Mrs. Tyson responded. The woman patted her shoulders once again and went on down the hall. Mrs. Tyson had heard that the woman was to be deported back to her home country. She must have gotten a reprieve somehow.

Mrs. Tyson wheeled back down the hall to the entrance to the nave. She would watch the end of the service, the procession out, and perhaps greet the clergy as they exited the service.

A baby cried during the last prayers, and Tabitha emerged from the side aisle with her baby boy in tow, a pacifier stuck in his mouth. "Aunt Eugenia! I'm so glad you made it!"

"Wouldn't' miss it for the world, darlin'."

"Thank you so much for the white prayer shawl. I knitted a blue one for him before we brought him home, but it's so special to have a family heirloom for the baptism."

"Prayer shawl?"

"The blanket your mother knitted. That's not what it is?"

Mrs. Tyson thought for a moment. "Well, now, I suppose it is. Mother knitted with lots of love. I suppose that's what makes it a prayer shawl."

At that moment, the ushers flung open the doors to the nave, and the acolytes appeared in front of Mrs. Tyson, the huge brass cross and the church banners held high. Tabitha stepped aside with the baby, leaving Mrs. Tyson surrounded by the choir, the priests, and the processional cross held above her.

Father Henderson bent down to kiss her on the cheek as the hymn ended.

"Go forth to love and serve the Lord, in the name of Jesus Christ," he called out to the congregation.

"Alleluia, Alleluia," Mrs. Tyson called out, adding her voice, once more, to the church she loved.

Next Chapters

Outside the church, the trees sported shimmering leaves of gold, red, and brown. A few black-eyed Susans still popped with yellow and black color in the flower beds alongside the walking trail. Tagging along behind Gus, Ginger squinted against the sunshine and enjoyed the slight chill against her cheeks in the fall air.

A year and a half had passed since she had first begun her walks in the Healing Garden of All Saints. She had thought about attending the service this morning, thinking perhaps she might sneak Gus into the Sunday service for the first time. But as the church bell rang, calling parishioners to prayer, Ginger decided her prayer best took place outside in the fresh air, getting some exercise and resting her mind.

Rounding the far end of the walking trail, Gus stopped for a comfort break. Ginger looked across the grounds to the high cross on the top of the church building. Her life had changed since she ducked out of the rain that first Wednesday, finding herself attending the Blessing of the Prayer Shawls service. She had healed. She had learned to knit. And she had settled into a new life and gone back to work.

She missed her old life, her old flooded-out farmhouse. But in the last six months, she had put that life behind her and transitioned into her new home here. Finally, by sitting and knitting by the windows overlooking the Tennessee River every time it rained, she felt secure. Her home wouldn't get washed out by a storm. She wouldn't have to move again unless she wanted to.

She had eventually applied for jobs and got one downtown, also in a building high on a bluff and nowhere near a flood plain. The time off to heal, as much as she had needed it, had come to an end. Now she needed the quiet again, at least on the weekends. She found herself coming back to All Saints again and again, but only to spend some "me time" walking with Gus in the healing garden. The people at All Saints had helped her heal, but she needed to move on.

Ginger let Gus meander along the trail a bit longer. While he sniffed at a hole in the ground, the thought occurred to Ginger that the church was like a train station. People moved through it, on their way to someplace else. Maybe you got a good meal at the station. Maybe you rested up for the next leg of the journey. Maybe you just got some supplies and a good book to read during your trip.

Ginger continued her walk. It was okay, something told her. She smiled and breathed in the crisp fall air as she walked along the path behind her dog.

On the opposite side of the healing garden, Nan sat on a bench, knitting a prayer shawl in greens and browns. She also had intended to go to the Sunday worship service. But as she approached the front door, a crisp breeze blew a bit of debris into her eye, causing tears to run down one side of her face. She stepped aside to pull herself together, right as the church bell rang to start off the service. By the time the debris had worked itself out of Nan's eye, the processional hymn and ended, and only the faint words of the new rector's prayer could be heard outside the nave.

Nan looked around her, at the vivid colors of the changing season and the full sunshine of a perfect autumn day. A wooden bench in the healing garden practically begged her to take a seat and spend some time outdoors. With unaccustomed guilt, Nan decided to try, just once, skipping the service and spending time with God alone, with her knitting instead of her prayer book.

She pulled out a prayer shawl project she had just started. Mercifully, she had stuffed it into her scuffed handbag just before leaving that morning. She couldn't imagine doing this – playing hooky from church – without something at least marginally prayerful to do.

Nan knit slowly, listening to the clack-clack of her wooden needles against the background of the fall leaves rustling in the wind. A woman wearing a brown barn jacket, walking a big reddish-brown dog, walked by, smiled in faint recognition, and continued on. Nan returned the smile, glad she hadn't stopped for a conversation. Nan felt her soul ascend into a state of meditation, a state of quiet joy.

She wondered where this prayer shawl would end up. Abby, the former associate priest at All Saints, had emailed her last week to tell her a wild, highly improbable story about seeing a photo of one of Nan's prayer shawls wrapped around a woman in Kenya. Abby claimed the woman had worn the shawl while collecting a donated chicken from an aid society, and one of the aid workers noticed the small tag attached to the shawl, labelling it as a gift of All Saints Church in Knoxville. In the photo, Abby claimed, you could just barely see the logo of the church prayer shawl ministry, the one Melba Strickland had commissioned to make sure people knew where the prayer shawls had come from.

Nan shook her head in amazement. That prayer shawl she had knit, probably during one of the Sunday morning services, had made its way all the way across the world to Africa.

"Maybe you should get out more, too." Nan heard these words almost as if someone standing beside her had spoken out loud.

Well, maybe I should, Nan thought. She knitted a few more rows, then stuck her prayer shawl project back in her old handbag and got up to leave. She couldn't help feeling a new life had begun.

Readers' Discussion Guide

Discussing a book with friends helps you share insights you've gained and learn from others as well. Reading is interactive, and as individuals, we all get something different from reading the same book or story. Talking about books and stories often inspires us to share our own stories, too, creating stronger bonds of friendship and community.

Here are questions you might use with friends, your book club, your knitting or prayer shawl group, or any small group meeting or discussion group:

Casting On (Icebreakers):

What was your favorite story in this book?

Which character did you like the best or identify with?

Work in Progress (Further Discussion):

Which story challenged your thinking, and why?

Which story helped you understand someone different from yourself?

Which story helped inspire you to do something new or different in your life or in your community?

Tying Up Loose Ends (Wrapping Up Your Discussion):

Which characters would you have included in the final "Next Chapters"?

What character would you like to know more about?

Additional Questions for Knitting Or Prayer Shawl Groups:

Why do you knit?

Which knitter in this book reminded you of yourself?

Have you ever knitted for charity? Did you give your knitting anonymously, and why or why not?

How does giving away your knitting change you?

What was the reaction of the person who received the gift of your knitting?

How is your story "looped together" with those to whom you give your knitting?

Additional Questions for Faith Formation Groups:

Did any of these stories remind you of any parables or other stories from the Bible? What was similar or different?

Did the church in this book remind you of your own faith community? What was different or the same?

Did any of these stories inspire you to do a new or different ministry?

What was your most important take-away from this book?

What insight would you most like to share with your faith community?

Acknowledgements

My profound thanks to all those who have nurtured my faith during the years preceding the writing of this book. All of the experiences, thoughts, and premises of each of these short stories are derived from my participation in Christian community, both in Knoxville and in the wider church.

My deep thanks to my husband, Tom, who has patiently read and commented so constructively on this manuscript and on all my books. He has a good eye for editing, and he's one of the few people in my life who will give me kind but honest feedback on my books.

I would also like to acknowledge all those who knit, crochet, or weave prayer shawls. I hope that this book will honor and affirm all the hours and hard work these crafters prayerfully dedicate in service to those in all kinds of need.

About the Author

Cynthia Coe is a writer based on her farm outside Knoxville, Tennessee and the mother of three children, two cats, and a dog. In between writing books and blog posts, she knits prayer shawls, hats, scarves, and the occasional sweater.

A graduate of Virginia Theological Seminary, she most recently served as a Justice & Advocacy Fellow of The Episcopal Church. She wrote the resources **Earth Our Garden Home, Wild Faith**, and **Considering Birds & Lilies** as part of this fellowship.

Her previously published fiction includes **Ginger's Reckoning** and **Runaway Kitty**, both available in paperback and e-book editions.

For more information or to contact the author, please visit www.sycamorecove.org or email sycamorecovecreations@gmail.com.

Made in the USA
Monee, IL
13 December 2022